BRAZEN RUSTLERS

"It's those men," Tony said, her voice tight with anger. "The ones we saw at the gather, rebranding my cattle."

Clint was watching the three men closely, yet with his vision wide, missing nothing: not the twitch on the big foreman's big face, nor the frozen grin on the pockmarked man, nor the sudden movement of the third man's hand, the one with the broken nose.

"Don't reach, mister," Clint ordered. "I can outdraw any of you."

"There is three of us," the foreman said, snarling the words.

"Then I'll only need three bullets, and I've got six."

The Gunsmith by J.R. Roberts

MACKLIN'S WOMEN
THE CHINESE GUNMAN
BULLETS AND BALLOTS
THE RIVERBOAT GANG
KILLER GRIZZLY
NORTH OF THE BORDER
EAGLE'S GAP
CHINATOWN HELL
THE PANHANDLE SEARCH
WILDCAT ROUNDUP
THE PONDEROSA WAR
TROUBLE RIDES A FAST HORSE
DYNAMITE JUSTICE
THE POSSE
NIGHT OF THE GILA
THE BOUNTY WOMEN
BLACK PEARL SALOON
WILD BILL'S GHOST
THE MINER'S SHOWDOWN
ARCHER'S REVENGE
SHOWDOWN IN RATON
WHEN LEGENDS MEET
DESERT HELL
THE DIAMOND GUN
DENVER DUO
HELL ON WHEELS
THE LEGEND MAKER
WALKING DEAD MAN
CROSSFIRE MOUNTAIN
THE DEADLY HEALER
THE TRAIL DRIVE WAR
GERONIMO'S TRAIL
THE COMSTOCK GOLD FRAUD
TEXAS TRACKDOWN
THE FAST DRAW LEAGUE
SHOWDOWN IN RIO MALO
OUTLAW TRAIL
HOMESTEADER GUNS
FIVE CARD DEATH
TRAILDRIVE TO MONTANA
TRIAL BY FIRE

THE OLD WHISTLER GANG
DAUGHTER OF GOLD
APACHE GOLD
PLAINS MURDER
DEADLY MEMORIES
THE NEVADA TIMBER WAR
NEW MEXICO SHOWDOWN
BARBED WIRE AND BULLETS
DEATH EXPRESS
WHEN LEGENDS DIE
SIX-GUN JUSTICE
MUSTANG HUNTERS
TEXAS RANSOM
VENGEANCE TOWN
WINNER TAKE ALL
MESSAGE FROM A DEAD MAN
RIDE FOR VENGEANCE
THE TAKERSVILLE SHOOT
BLOOD ON THE LAND
SIX-GUN SHOWDOWN
MISSISSIPPI MASSACRE
THE ARIZONA TRIANGLE
BROTHERS OF THE GUN
THE STAGECOACH THIEVES
JUDGMENT AT FIRECREEK
DEAD MAN'S JURY
HANDS OF THE STRANGLER
NEVADA DEATH TRAP
WAGON TRAIN TO HELL
RIDE FOR REVENGE
DEAD RINGER
TRAIL OF THE ASSASSIN
SHOOT-OUT AT CROSSFORK
BUCKSKIN'S TRAIL
HELLDORADO
THE HANGING JUDGE
THE BOUNTY HUNTER
TOMBSTONE AT LITTLE HORN
KILLER'S RACE
WYOMING RANGE WAR
GRAND CANYON GOLD

THE GUNSMITH

#112

GUNS DON'T ARGUE

SPEAKING VOLUMES, LLC
NAPLES, FLORIDA
2016

THE GUNSMITH
#112 GUNS DON'T ARGUE

ISBN 978-1-61232-715-0

For more exciting
Books, eBooks, Audiobooks and more visit us at
www.speakingvolumes.us

THE GUNSMITH

#112

GUNS DON'T ARGUE

J.R. ROBERTS

Chapter One

There must have been a first person to remark that Kansas sod held more water than any other part of the United States, that the climate had changed in Kansas and that the breaking of the sod had increased the retention of moisture.

At any rate, Clint Adams had heard the remark more than a few times—in Dodge, in Wichita, Abilene, in Kansas City. It was the kind of statement that smelled suspiciously of land-grabber bunco. And for some reason he didn't care to pursue, it had come into his thoughts now on his way north and west toward Plains, the town in which he expected to see his old friend Hank Sayles.

He had crossed the Arkansas River at Turnbow Junction and recrossed it at Ember. Now, in the middle of the hot forenoon, he studied the distance: the long flat prairie, dry as a dead man's breath, as an old-timer had once put it. He sat atop Duke, his big black gelding, his eyes slowly sweeping the great robe of tawny-colored

1

buffalo grass, with no more shade to protect him than that thrown by the brim of his Stetson.

It was then he spotted them. They were riding fine horses—he could tell even at that distance. One a big gray, a bit hammerheaded, the other a rangy sorrel with a wide white blaze and three white stockings. They were a lean pair, each riding with the same arrogance and packing hardware. At that distance he couldn't see their faces, yet he could read them. He could read the atmosphere that rode with them.

They were soon out of sight; he was certain they had not seen him. As far as he could tell, they must have crossed the river off to his right, not far from the thick butte that rose like a tower from the sparse land surrounding it. Well, he reasoned, they appeared to be heading in the same direction as himself, so he kicked Duke into a brisk walk and pointed him toward the big butte.

An hour later he caught the sound of the cattle. They were on the far side of the butte, and he knew he was nearing water. So did Duke. He had lifted his head, perking right up at the smell of something cool to drink, something cool on his legs. And shortly, finding the ford across the river, they stopped to let the water swirl around the big gelding's feet and the lower part of his legs.

Clint Adams, having carefully studied his surroundings, now removed his big hat and, bending far down from his saddle with a good grip on his saddle horn, scooped water into the wide brim and raised it to his mouth. It was cold, sparkling in the sunlight, and in the shallow place where they were he could see clearly to the bed of the river.

Now he took some water in his hand and ran it over his hot face. Duke by now had had his fill, and they crossed to the far side of the river. Coming up on the hot prairie, the man known as the Gunsmith drew rein.

The bawling of the cattle grew louder. As he walked his horse forward, he saw a faint cloud of dust rising off to his left from the other side of a thick row of box elders. And he could hear the men. He knew there would probably be outriders, holding the herd while the men branded. For it was obviously a branding party. What wasn't so obvious, though, was the quality of welcome that might be offered. Quickly now, he turned Duke and they cantered toward some cottonwoods that ran along the edge of what looked to be a draw. The Gunsmith was looking for a spot from which he could see what was going on without himself being seen.

In a few minutes he had ridden along the side of the draw and come to a line of trees that protected him from being seen, while at the same time affording him a clear view of the action below, in the belly of the long, low, wide draw.

There must have been four dozen beeves in the gather. And Clint counted a dozen hands. But it wasn't a regular branding by any means. There were two men roping on horseback, though only one fire for the branding irons. The size of the herd, which was small, the number of men, plus two ropers told him this was no orthodox branding. He would have bet what he owned that those irons were running irons, the kind that could change a brand to what suited the animal's new owner.

And then, as though to verify his view, he saw the hammerhead gray and the three-stocking sorrel he'd spotted earlier—with, it looked like, their same riders. He could see their faces now. One was badly pockmarked, while the other had a broken nose.

The men were calling back and forth as they worked, but he couldn't make out what they were saying. He didn't feel the need to. The scene spoke for itself. And there was no point in his staying there. It was just as he decided to turn around and continue on his way that he heard the horse somewhere in back of him.

Quickly he dismounted and led Duke into the stand of trees to his right; and then, holding his hand over his mount's muzzle so he wouldn't nicker in recognition to the approaching horse and rider, he waited.

Had he been spotted? He was pretty sure not. He'd been careful. He always was. And in this instance, with a band of obvious hardcases below him, he wasn't going to loosen his attention. It sounded like just the one horse, and the rider was not moving with much caution. He felt the agitation in the evident haste with which the horseman was approaching the edge of the draw. He was now sure it wasn't one of the branding bunch but someone quite else. Maybe the rightful owner of the cattle, was the thought that crossed his mind.

The Gunsmith was used to surprises, and these were not always pleasant. All the same, he wasn't quite ready for the wonder that swept through him as the little roan came through the widely spaced trees. Yet it was not the roan that was the surprise, but its rider. No lean, gun-hipped saddle rover but a lovely, well-formed, chestnut-haired young woman beneath a soft brown Stetson, with the biggest brown eyes he thought he'd ever seen, the most appealing mouth, plus a figure that seemed almost an integral part of the roan horse, sitting that agile animal as though she were growing right out of the saddle.

Nor was he prepared for her first utterance.

"What are you doing here?" And he noted how she caught her breath, as though she wasn't used to the role of interrogation, yet was managing it well enough.

"I am minding my own business," the Gunsmith said.

"I am doing the same, since this happens to be my land, and I am repeating my question: Who are you, and what are you doing here?" She spoke firmly, though without hostility.

"I'm passing through," Clint said. "You got anything against that?"

"You're connected with those men?" She nodded in the direction of the branding. "You can ride down there and tell Mr. Slade that I have sent to the army for the law. And I will have him and his men arrested for what they're doing, and for what they have already done."

He noticed then the anger standing in her huge, dark brown eyes.

"I am not connected with those men," Clint said. "My name is Clint Adams, and I am just passing through. I don't know those men, and I don't want to know them. Now, believe me or not; it's your deal."

She continued to stare at him, nonplussed. Clearly, she half believed him and half didn't. But he felt she somehow wanted to believe what he was saying.

"You're not one of Slade's men?"

"Nope."

"Are you the new marshal?"

"Sorry."

"You're . . . "

"Just passing through." And he touched the brim of his hat with his left forefinger, still holding his reins in the same hand, and walked the big black closer. "Sorry, miss. I'm a stranger to this country."

She said nothing. She sat her pony, a little less tense now, her dark eyes regarding him seriously.

"It might be a good notion to get out of here," Clint said, in a tone of voice that suddenly took charge of the situation. "Maybe sooner than later, one of those wranglers from down there will come up and see that he and his outfit are not alone. I don't think it would be healthy for either one of us to be caught up in that kind of thing."

"Those are my cattle," she said, the words coming out fast. "At least some are. I am dead sure of that. I had wished you were the marshal, but then I didn't see any badge on you, so I took you to be one of them. I am sorry."

"What would you have done if I had been . . . one of them?" Clint asked as he kneed Duke forward and nodded his head for both of them to leave.

"I don't know," she said, turning the roan. "I might have had to shoot you."

"You would? How?"

"With my gun," she said, raising the derringer that she'd been holding just behind the pommel of her saddle.

"I'm glad you didn't try," the Gunsmith said.

"So am I. I wouldn't really have wanted to shoot you."

"It wasn't for that I'm glad you didn't try," Clint said easily.

"For what then?" And she turned her head as their

horses, which were now alongside each other, left the area.

"Because then I would have had to shoot you," the Gunsmith said simply. "And I wouldn't have cared for that."

Her eyes were huge as she turned to face him. "You mean you really—really—would!"

"It was obvious from the first moment I saw you that you had a gun there back of your pommel. From the way you were setting your saddle."

"But . . . "

"I think it's time to change the conversation," the Gunsmith said. "If you don't live too far from here, miss, I would sure favor a good cup of coffee and maybe a biscuit or two."

Clint Adams decided that Fate—or whatever force it was that was in operation at the time—had smiled on him. His new companion was delightful. The right height, width, character—everything. She needed nothing; other than possibly himself, he swiftly decided. And at her cabin—or ranch house, as she called it—he enjoyed two excellent mugs of coffee.

Her name was Tony—Antonia Miller—and she lived alone with a young brother of twelve, who at the moment was helping out at one of the neighboring ranches in the valley. Horseshoe Valley encompassed the Tall Bull River, which was a fast-running, winding rush of water pouring down from the mountains, through the Horseshoe between high rimrocks, on its way to Alder Crossing.

She told him she'd been born in the house in which they were having coffee. "My mom died when I was real young, while she was giving birth to Andy."

"And your dad?" Clint asked, realizing her sudden hesitation but deciding to ask her anyway. For he was charmed by her open manner. The lobes of her ears showed just below her chestnut hair, just enough to bring a pounding in his chest, and as his eyes felt over her bosom—when she had at one point turned away to check the coffeepot—an even stronger thumping began in the region of his crotch. At one particular moment, when she got up to fetch something and the sunlight caught her hair as it came through the kitchen window, he thought how she was truly part of that long, wide-open valley. Clearly, it was her home, in every sense of the word.

He kept congratulating himself on his good fortune in meeting her and wondered whether she had a husband or someone special "dancing attendance on her," as the writer of a magazine article he'd recently read had put it.

"My dad's dead. He just up and got the croup one day," she said simply. She had lowered her head and was looking down at her hands, which were together in her lap.

He watched her knuckles whiten as she said those words.

"I'm sorry." And then he said quickly. "And now you and Andy take care of the ranch."

She nodded, still with her head bowed. "We do."

"But somebody has been rustling your stock."

"Those men. I've ordered them off our land. But I might as well whistle in the wind."

"Is it one outfit, or more?" he asked.

"Mostly Slade. Asa Slade. I don't know why he can't leave us alone. He's already got heaven knows how much acreage in the valley. And cattle."

"Isn't there any law about?"

"There was."

"I see."

Suddenly she raised her head, and he saw that her eyes were clear, and she was even smiling in a shy way. "I am sorry to let our conversation get gloomy. You see, I had thought when I first saw you that you might be one of Slade's men. Then I thought, too, you might be the new marshal I wrote for to Fort Wilby."

The Gunsmith opened his hands, palms up. "Sorry, but I don't fill the bill either way."

"Well anyway, that's how it is. Now that's all settled; who I am and what I'm doing."

"What are you doing?" he asked. "That is, what are you planning to do now?"

"I will fight them. I don't have a plan. But I will fight them. I'll do more than that. That I promise!"

He saw the flash in her eyes, the set of her face. And still, hard as she suddenly became, he saw that she was still beautiful.

"Don't you have anyone to help you?"

"I've a cousin in Minnesota, and I've written, inviting him out. But I've heard nothing."

"My next question is, Why not sell the place? But I guess I can answer that myself."

She nodded. "Would you sell it if you were in my shoes?"

He grinned at that and said nothing.

"How about another coffee?"

"I'll start turning brown. But you sure know how to boil up a fine pot."

She was already pouring, while he reached for another biscuit.

"Now and again I do get help from the outfit across the river; old man Sargent and sometimes Billy and Martha Wells come by and give a hand. They live downriver. You'll pass them on the way to Alder. I mean, if that's where you're heading."

"I was heading for Plains," Clint said.

"Same place. Plains used to be Alder. Dad and some others never did get to accepting the new name. So I guess I just grew up calling it Alder. I suppose I'd better get in step with the rest of the country," she added wryly.

"I'm a gunsmith," Clint said. "I left my wagon and team back at Wichita. They slow me down actually; anyway, I had some time on my hands and thought I'd mosey along here and on up to Wyoming and maybe Idaho. I can always pick up tools if I need 'em."

"You mend—repair—guns."

He nodded. "You got anything needs fixing?"

"Only that window there, which I cannot open."

He was already on his feet.

"I didn't mean for you to . . . "

But he had already reached the window and was inspecting it. "You got a hammer, a chisel? It's swollen. I'll trim it down, and that ought to do her. And some grease," he added.

It didn't take him long to get the window so it opened and closed easily. "Logs settled on 'er," he explained, cleaning up some of the wood shavings.

He saw that she was about to say something, when suddenly they heard the horses. They were coming in fast.

She was at the window instantly.

"Keep to the side," he said, loosening his holster and checking his six-gun for an easy draw.

"It's those men," she said, her voice tight with anger. "The ones at the gather."

He had stepped across the room to another window. "How many?"

"Three."

"Well, they've surely spotted my horse, so they know you're not alone."

She had started toward the door, but he stopped her. "Let me talk to them."

"No. No—but thank you. It's my fight. Why Mr. Adams, I hardly know you. I can't ask you to—"

Her words were cut off by the big voice coming through the closed door, as somebody knocked loudly.

"In there! Tony Miller, this is Butch Holmes, foreman of the ZT Bar. We found eight ZT beeves in your herd, and we cut 'em out and rebranded 'em. Mr. Slade is warning you not to do any more rustling, or you're going to be in real trouble!" Those words were followed by a great thump on the door, as though from a rifle butt.

During this conversation, Clint had found the back door and slipped outside. He rounded the front corner of the cabin, catching the big man as he turned his horse. The three riders, caught by surprise, all spun to face him.

"So that's your big black!" snapped the biggest of the three. He was obviously the man who had shouted through the door, the leader.

The Gunsmith waited a beat, and with his words coming out even as a milled board, he said, "That is my horse, the same I'll be riding out to inspect your branding job."

He was watching them closely, yet with his vision wide, missing nothing: not the twitch on the big foreman's face, nor the frozen grin on the pockmarked man, nor the sudden movement of the third man's hand, the one with the broken nose.

"Don't reach, mister. I can outdraw any of you."

"There is three of us," the foreman said, snarling the words.

"Then I'll only need three bullets, and I've got six. Now git!"

Someone started to move as his horse took a step forward, but Holmes, the foreman, spoke up quickly.

"Cole!"

"We can take him, Butch."

"Not now. We got our orders, and you got yours. I'll tell you when it's necessary to draw."

Butch Holmes was a square-shouldered man, built like a box. He spat over his horse's withers now, squinting down at the man who had challenged them.

A moment passed, while one of the horses nickered.

Then Holmes said, "That there is a neat hoss you got, mister, I'd sure hate to see anything happen to him."

"That is what I know," the Gunsmith said. "Because then you'd be dealing with me."

He remained standing there, his eyes following them as they rode out of sight.

When he came back into the cabin, he found her standing by the kitchen stove, peering out the window. He could see the tension in her body.

"Thank you," she said.

And suddenly she was in his arms, her head against his chest, as the tears shook her.

It only lasted a moment, and then she pulled herself together and stepped back from him. "I'm sorry. Forgive me, for . . . for . . . "

"For being human? Don't be silly. You're a very brave person," he said. "Would you like me to stay through the night? I can, very easily."

"Thank you. Thank you. But I'll be all right. And Andy will be home soon."

"I'll be heading into Plains then."

"I am very grateful, Mr. Adams."

"Clint."

Suddenly she smiled. "And I am Tony."

He grinned at her. "You know something, miss? That's just who I thought you were."

"Tony," she repeated. "Not miss."

"Sorry." Then, mischievously: "I mean, Tony."

Her laugh was delightful.

"Do you have schoolmarm blood in your veins, Tony?"

"Have you got schoolboy?"

"Sure have."

And they both chuckled over that, while he continued to admire the curve of her cheek, the dancing that had suddenly swung into her eyes, her nearness as she reached over to pick up his mug for more coffee.

Chapter Two

At precisely high noon on a fine spring day, Clint Adams pushed open the doors of the Ever & Always Best Saloon in Plains. And also at that precise moment, a short man dressed in solemn black climbed onto the bar and held up his hands, shouting, "Quiet, gents!"

The Gunsmith took in the situation at a glance. Indeed, there wasn't that much room for anything more. The place was packed to the four walls with men, all evidently wearing guns. All eyes were trained right on the little man standing on the bar.

Suddenly a big bruiser standing near Clint bellowed belligerently, "Let's cut the shit, mister, and bring out them women! I mean right now!" He looked around the room. "I mean, what the hell we waitin' fer!"

A roar greeted this gingery salutation, but the small man standing on the bar didn't blink. Obviously, he knew his business.

"Now don't go gettin' yerselves all horned up and

ornery, boys. All I'm intending to say is that the women
will be coming out pronto, and I am saying for you kindly
not to feel, squeeze, pinch, stroke, fondle, tickle, or in any
way handle 'em if you ain't got the cartwheels to bid.
These here are high-class ladies from the best families
back East, and it makes them nervous to have any horsin'
around. I mean, if a man ain't being serious about his
future wife . . . "

He nodded his small bare head a couple of times in
emphasis of this interesting declaration, ran his forefinger
down the side of his long nose, then jumped down from
the bar—nearly falling, but regaining himself with the
help of an anonymous hand. And then, with his hands
gripping the lapels of his black coat, he shrugged the
garment into a better fit over his thin shoulders and, with
his head leading the way, marched rapidly toward a door
at the rear of the saloon. All eyes followed him as the
crowd parted like the sea to allow important passage. A
low murmuring accompanied him.

In only moments he returned, leading a dozen women
of various shape, size, and age. He lined his charges up
at the bar, then climbed back up to stand on top of the
long mahogany structure, which was amply dotted with
glasses of whiskey.

There was no need this time for him to hold up his
hands for silence. No one had anything to say. No one
would have dared disturb that pregnant moment. Clint
noted that there were more than just a few jaws that had
dropped open in respect for the awesome event.

The auctioneer nodded now toward one of the women
who were lined up. "All right then, Connie Mae. Come
on up here and let the gents have a look at you!" Reach-

ing down, he took the hand of a faded, heavyset blonde with a very round face, big bosom, and large behind.

Standing beside Mr. Harvey Whent, she bounced her hips just a mite and lisped, "Pleased to meet yah all!"

Clint Adams could see that her main offering was an obvious lasciviousness and practice in the exercise of same.

A howl of appreciation went up from a number of throats. A middle-aged rancher with a scar along the left side of his face suddenly whipped out his six-shooter and shouted, "By jingo, that there is a piece of woman! I am bidding one hundred dollars right now. I say, right now! And don't anybody even dast to bid otherways. I mean, like, agin me!"

A younger man, however, was not dismayed by this announcement, nor even by the drawn revolver—liquor as usual having its say—and instantly bid a hundred and fifty dollars.

The first man, who Clint learned later was named Henderson, roared with rage. "You buy yourself somebody else, you puppy dog. This here woman is mine! And right now. I got one hunnert says so on the barrelhead, and I got this here piece to back it, by jingo!" And he drew back the hammer on his six-gun.

But indiscretion, fueled by booze and passion, prevailed, and the young man foolishly reached for his own weapon. He was met by the slug of Mr. Henderson's Colt, which kicked once—all that was necessary. The young man who had challenged the older didn't even clear leather. He was dead.

Suddenly the big bruiser standing near Clint who had challenged the auctioneer to get on with things now decided that Connie Mae was just the wife for him. Without even a word of warning, he drew his holstered handgun and cut Henderson to the floor.

"I am bidding a hundred and forty dollars for that pretty gal. And that is it!" His words were as hard as his bullet had been.

Connie Mae was smiling as she stepped down from the bar, revealing a tasty length of leg as she did so. Two men killed for her; well, it was something to write home about, the Gunsmith was reflecting, as he watched the young lady's husband-to-be slip his big arm around his "property."

Mr. Harvey Whent, flushed with the success of his first offering, waited only for the two bodies to be removed, and then he turned to his women standing at the back of the bar. "Melanie, you're next," he said to a shapely redhead who looked to be in her early twenties.

Whent reached down and grasped Melanie's hand and pulled her up onto the bar. She was cute. Coy. Her smile brought a roar of glee from the crowded room, but when she lifted her dress a couple of inches above her knees, the crowd was all at once stunned into silence. Then a murmuring started that so bold a woman would never be the kind a man could trust when he was away from home. Whent hissed, glaring at the girl. "Stop playing the whore. This place ain't Denver. These hicks, they're not the sort you bin screwing, dammit. They're looking for wives. Now stand still and quit wiggling your ass and try to look decent!"

The crowd was not so interested in Melanie. There was no shooting, and when a farmer finally bid a hundred for her, Whent swiftly closed the deal.

Clint continued to hang around, and within another hour and a half, Whent had auctioned off the rest of his women.

The crowd had thinned at the Ever & Always Best Saloon and Clint Adams moved to the bar. He had just ordered another drink, having nursed only one during the entire auction, when he first felt, then heard the step off his right side and behind him.

"I generally like strangers in town to check in with my office." The voice was stern, gravelly with authority, but it didn't sound mean to Clint Adams. He turned to face the bony man wearing the star on his dark, sweat-stained shirt and remembered Tony Miller telling him there was no law in Plains.

"Specially when they be wearing hardware," the man with the tin badge continued.

"I would have looked you up, Marshal, excepting I'd been told there was no lawman in Plains. I'm just what you see here. My name is Clint Adams, and I make a habit of calling on the law when I hit town. Used to be a lawman myself."

"I know who you be, mister. Read the papers on you, some of them wild stories, and I hear talk."

Clint shrugged pleasantly in the face of this information, which he'd had to confront often enough already in his young life.

"I ain't pushing you. Just letting you know I'm about."

"Appreciate it, Marshal."

"The name is Studley." Then he added, "Got my appointment yestiddy. Acting Marshal."

"Noble Studley. I've heard of you," Clint said. "Good things," he quickly added.

"Good or bad, that is done for now, whatever it was."
Marshal Studley nodded at the barkeep, who brought a
bottle and glass and placed it before him.

He was a lanky man, Studley. Clint Adams noted that
his eyes were a different color from each other, one blu-
ish yellow, the other greenish blue. He was cleanshaven,
and there were deep crow's feet under his eyes, reaching
to his high cheekbones. Clint wondered if he had Indian
blood. He had big knuckles on his big hands and prominent wristbones. He was surprised at the lawman's next
words: "You work on gun fixin', do you."

Clint nodded. "You got anything needs work?"

"Might." Marshal Noble Studley's words were slightly
muffled, for he was saying them into his glass of whiskey
as he lifted it to drink.

They were silent a moment, and then Studley said,
"Well, I'll say welcome to Plains, Adams. We're a building town. Like you can see."

"That's what I've been hearing," Clint said. "There's
a lot of welcome, and building talk to boot."

"Folks'll be after you to settle." He leaned closer.
"Like I say, I have heard of you. I know about you.
And what I hear is good. You got a real fast gun, but
you don't look for trouble, exceptin' when it comes you
ain't settin' there pickin' yer nose."

"I try to keep my nose clean," the Gunsmith said, picking right up on the marshal's quaint observation. "Anyhow, I'm glad to be in Plains."

The marshal leaned even closer now, though not
apparently so. It was an extremely slight movement,
and therefore, Clint realized it had to be freighted with
something special.

"They're fixin' to make Plains the county seat." Studley's words were almost a whisper, and the Gunsmith wondered why. He said so.

"Why? Is that a secret or something?"

"Ain't no secret," Studley replied, straightening up. "It's just that when people get to talkin' about it, they get theirselves all riled on it. We've had some shootings like that. See, there's Mile Butte." And he jerked his thumb over his shoulder. "They figure they oughtta be county seat."

"And they're fixing to maybe fight over it?" Clint asked, as his eyes took in the roomful of drinkers at the Ever & Always Best Saloon.

"Money. Land. The railroad, mebbe. But let me tell you, you could do a whole helluva lot worse than settle in Plains. Why, Plains is just about the best little town this side of the Mississippi, and likely on th'other side, too."

And suddenly the marshal of Plains slapped his big hand down onto the mahogany bar and let out a Texas cowboy yell that brought the whole barroom off its heels.

"Men, I want you to meet Mr. Clint Adams. He is passing through, or maybe he ain't. Maybe he likes this place. Maybe we can talk him into stopping here, settling. Becoming a citizen of our fair town, our clean, honest, God-fearing community! What d'ya say, Mr. Adams?"

Clint had felt the initial shock rush through his body like a juggernaut. The lawman's sudden switch from his taciturn manner to a town and county booster was indeed astonishing. Still, in his line of work the Gunsmith was used to shocks, and so he took his role: the role of a possible settler in the citizens' fair town. And the drinks flowed across the bar, the talk got louder, and the Gunsmith kept his attention at razor's edge, for he just felt in the very marrow of his bones that something was going to happen, either soon or late.

Presently, Marshal Noble Studley polished off his drink, nodded to Clint, and turned and left the saloon, leaving the Gunsmith more or less surrounded by a bibulous group of town and county-seat boosters who were proclaiming the advantages of living in Plains and, in particular, the need to live in Plains rather than Mile Butte.

The auctioneer extraordinary, as he saw himself, Mr. Harvey Whent, sat grinning in his room at the K.C. House. He was grinning all over himself, for, unlike his former schemes, which he had plied over most of the West, in this one his marks were glad to part with their money. Indeed, he was performing a Great Service for the community. The crowd had as good as said so. They wanted more—more women!—the scarcity in the West being painful. And he had promised another visit. Although he was thinking that it would be better to try some other hamlet for his unique enterprise: the shipment of wives to the lonely men of the frontier. After all, it was scarcity that made the market go. And he saw clearly that he had plenty of work lying ahead. His grin widened.

He was sitting on his bed, counting his take for the second time—it was a delicious feeling!—when there came a pounding on the door.

Swiftly he swept the money out of sight and called out, "Who is there?"

"It's the law! Open this door, 'fore I shoot the lock off!"

Harvey Whent felt an all-too-familiar chill run through him as he stood up and unlocked the door.

"You be under arrest," Marshal Noble Studley said as he stepped swiftly into the almost naked room.

"What for?" demanded the righteous Harvey Whent, thankful that he had whisked his money out of sight.

"For selling humans, mostly women, and also for having brung on the dee-mise of a couple other humans who wasn't even part of yer crooked scheme." His tone was heavy with Old Testament punishment. "Our fair town don't need this kind of scalawaggin'."

"I am innocent," declared the stunned Harvey Whent, his mind racing back to the time he'd played a justice of the peace somewhere along the Mississippi, searching for some kind of legal tongue-twister to throw the big boney bastard off the trail.

"You have got to have witnesses that I did any wrong," he said, speaking in his cleverest tone of voice.

"We got witnesses. I got 'em," the marshal corrected. "Plus two corpus delectuses. Mister, we got you by the balls!"

Harvey winced. "I am innocent," he protested again. "And I can prove my innocence. I was merely helping those poor young women to find themselves husbands, at the same time furnishing the lonely men of this forsaken part of our great country with young, healthy, hardworking wives. You dastard, sir, are you—"

"You little sonofabitch, don't you dast call me a bastard! Why, I'll whip your skinny ass from here to breakfast, by jingo!"

"I said *dastard*! Not *bastard*!"

Quicker than anything Harvey Whent had ever seen in

his forty-some years, that big hogleg was in the marshal's fist. Like it lived there!

"You kin argue it with the judge," Marshal Noble Studley said. "An' I don't give a shit what first letter you used on that word. Whatever it is, was, or is gonna be, you don't get away with callin' the law that; nor, most especially, you don't call it to Noble Studley, you little piss-ant!"

Harvey Whent, although thrown by this sudden, unexpected turn of events, was no amateur at his life's work. He rallied, his mind racing ahead to all possibilities that might help him extricate himself from this seeming disaster. And, being a professional, his thoughts fastened almost immediately onto the obvious.

"Marshal Studley, sir! I was not actually selling women. I was in fact just getting back some of what it cost me to bring them out from Kansas City and Denver, plus a few measly dollars for my time and trouble. Plus!" He raised his short forefinger, as it looked like the man of the law was going to interrupt. "Plus, I didn't kill anybody. I wasn't even wearing a gun; not even a toothpick. Those poor gents went to their maker courtesy of somebody other than Harvey Whent, sir. I mean, Marshal."

For a moment, this seemed to take the wind out of Studley. Yet he retreated without grace, stating harshly that if Whent ever again set foot in Plains with a load of whores, he'd blast him to Kingdom Come. And right now!

"I for sure ain't allowin' this fine town of Plains to come to a cesspool of sin on account of you and your ways of makin' easy money. Filthy money!" he added, fury lacing his words.

For an instant Harvey Whent had the idea that the marshal was trying to corner him into a gunfight. But he was not without courage, and his nimble mind had already worked out his plan, even while the angry lawman was churning the air in the tiny room with his fulmination against the evils of whoring, illicit moneymaking, antisocial fun, and the like.

"See, Marshal, it says in the Bible, like I am sure a man of your stature oughtta know—does know! It says a man ain't worth a hole in the wall without a woman."

"That's what I know," Studley said, taking a seat on the only chair in the room; it had a rung missing, so he sat down gingerly. "That's what I know," he repeated. "And I would guess a man like you can appreciate the position of a honest lawmen in respect to your noxious scheme."

"But you see, looking at the Good Book, Marshal Studley, a man such as yerself might come to figure as how I am actually doing the work of the Lord. After all, I am providin' womenless men with women. With wives, sir! Not concubines!"

The marshal's face creased painfully in thought at this—to him—surprising piece of logic.

"Never took a look at it that way," he admitted. "Course, it does mention that about women in the Bible, about a man needin' a woman."

"What I need, Marshal Studley, is a partner. Someone to help me with all the details, and there are many. Why, like I told you, I had to charge money for my services and all."

He paused, letting this bold stroke ease into the lawman. "You'd be performing a duty to the citizens of our Great West." The words slipped out of his mouth like melting butter. "And you'd also be making a few dollars for yerself." He watched his quarry carefully as he added, "And, oh, one thing more: Course, you'll also have the opportunity of having sex with all of them women on their way out here."

"That would not be right," the marshal said. "Sin is not my dish! I'm agin it. Besides, how'm I gonna give up my marshal's job? Took me a helluva long time and some greasing to get it, and I ain't anxious to dump it just like that." And then he stopped abruptly, evidently realizing he'd said just a little too much.

But Harvey Whent rode over his words with ease. "You wouldn't have to travel, then. You'd be here, like on the receivin' end. See, keep your job, and you can still exercise your right to have any of the women before they get sold—I mean, before they get auctioned. And you'd be keeping everything straight with the law, being as how you know all the ways of the law, and I wouldn't be breaking any of it. Plus, like I said, you could like see that the merchandise was good quality and none of the customers was getting cheated." He grinned, opening his hands, expansive as a man running for office. "See, you would be like the conscience of our enterprise, while I am filling a true need of the male population: helping to make them happy members of the flock of the Lord."

"It is still sinful. I mean, that last part."

Harvey could see that he was weakening, nonetheless. And he brought over his clincher. "Listen, when I tell those starving men—who haven't had a woman since the

Lord knows when—what a certain woman is worth, I got to know my material. I got to know what the hell I am talking about. Otherwise, I am misrepresenting, and *that* is going versus the law!"

A silence invaded the room at that point. And Harvey knew it was not the moment to press. He had said his piece—and done well, according to his reckoning. Now it was up to the lawman to take what was offered. By God, he had to! The man couldn't be that much of a fool, after all. Harvey waited, going back over what he had said to Studley, sure now that he'd done his best work. The man simply couldn't resist. Hell, a marshal's pay wouldn't buy a man a pot to piss in; everyone knew that. Studley simply had to go for it.

Meanwhile, the marshal of Plains had taken out his sack of tobacco and his papers and was building a cigarette. Harvey Whent knew that he was thinking. He watched the forefingers and thumbs loading and rolling the paper, and then he watched as Studley licked and sealed the cigarette, all in one smooth stroke, without a grain of wasted effort, without the loss of a shred of tobacco.

Reaching down, the marshal struck a wooden lucifer on his belt buckle and lit the cigarette.

But Harvey Whent was a man who had resources in depth. Just as he realized that his clincher hadn't quite won the day, a flash of what he later described to himself as heroic genius came to him. It was indeed heroic, and unalloyed as well, the thought coming even as he now spoke those decisive words.

"You can figure, too, how all those women coming in are maybe going to add to the population—will, in fact, add to it—thus giving more people to Plains than to Mile Butte."

"You be a man with the devil's tongue," Noble Studley said, in the clerical tone he appeared to favor when addressing matters of sex and such.

"I for one do see Plains as the better town for the county seat," the Great Entrepreneur said softly.

Marshal Studley's strangely colored eyes were strained in thought as he received this latest bit of artillery from the crisp little man seated on the edge of the bed.

"They'll be deciding on the county seat pretty directly," he said, the cigarette hanging on his lip and moving up and down in time with his words.

"The more reason then to come to an intelligent decision," Harvey pointed out, holding his eyes on the tip of the marshal's nose. He was also watching for the lengthening cigarette ash to fall.

"How long you figger till you can bring in another shipment?" Studley asked.

And without moving a single muscle in his face, Harvey Whent felt his smile of victory; and it was the sweetest, because known only to himself. He noted, too, that the ash had still not fallen from Noble Studley's cigarette. Clearly the marshal was steady, one of those men in whom one could feel a certain confidence.

The dining room in the K.C. House was deserted, save for the small party at one end of the room, plus Clint Adams at the other end, seated so that he was facing the open doorway and the lobby. At this off-hour of the afternoon, there were few diners.

Mr. Curfew Bakertone virtually never dined alone.

Invariably, as now he favored the support of at least one other person—even his wife—but more frequently upward to half a dozen kept him company.

Business was conducted at such gatherings; business and also "business"—those special one-to-one understandings—and there was also a good deal of bantering, jockeying for place, and combat in the various vulnerable zones of the sycophants. Praise was served from the head of the table, and there was ample skewering of underlings, so that the event was always something that was dreaded and at the same time looked forward to, Mr. Bakertone being a man of such high consequence.

He was, indeed, head of the New England Cattle, Land & Transportation Company. The New England had its main office in Boston and branch offices in New York, Cheyenne, and Kansas City. Its grasp was wide and notoriously firm. Now and again inquisitive persons had asked what such a personage as Curfew Bakertone was doing in such out-of-the-way places as Red River, Dole City, Gebo, and presently Plains and Mile Butte. But it was known that C.B. was a man who knew how to attend to detail.

Seated alone at the far corner of the room, the Gunsmith, upon learning who the cadaverous-looking old gent was, wasn't at all surprised. He had heard of Curfew Bakertone. He'd heard his name in Abilene, Casper, Pitchfork, Denver, Frisco, Fort Worth, Wichita, and more. And it was obvious that the man had reached his powerful financial position, not by counting his money behind a desk, but by getting out there and rolling up his sleeves, to outwork, outthink, outdo all and every kind of competition that came within his purview. Clearly, Mr. Bakertone was a man of action.

Clint Adams studied him now, using his newspaper as a foil. Once he caught the lean man looking in his direction, but he didn't hold his eyes; he dropped back into his paper. He was wondering what particular business Bakertone was up to in a tiny, dust-ridden, hole-in-the-ground, one-horse town like Plains. Surely, nothing to do with the county seat thing he'd been hearing about. Men such as Bakertone didn't grub for coins.

The Gunsmith began remembering things he had heard, but then he let it go. He was actually waiting for his friend Hank Sayles to meet him. Hank had written, suggesting Clint might drop by if he ever happened to be in that part of the country. The invite had been casual, but Clint Adams knew his old friend well enough to read the spaces and had come up with a more explicit purpose than mere socializing. Those spaces between the written words told the Gunsmith that his friend was in trouble.

Idly, he continued to scan the newspaper, but his attention was more and more drawn to the table where Curfew Bakertone was hosting a party of three other men. The conversation appeared quite ordinary; at that distance Clint could hear nothing, other than an occasional laugh and, at one point, an attack of coughing issuing from Bakertone himself.

Earlier he had left a note at Hank's office, which was on Main Street, saying that he was in town and would be at the K.C. House. He had supposed his friend, who had been a land surveyor when they'd known each other down in Ringley, Arizona, was still in that line of work.

And indeed, he was pleased to see Hank's name lettered on the sign outside his office, with the title "Land Surveyor" beneath it.

Clint had a full view of the door into the dining room, and he also had a clear view, though more distant, of the Bakertone table. It seemed a jolly group, though he noticed solemnity falling over the table every so often, usually when the reedy man of power was speaking. And he began speculating again.

He knew that Curfew Bakertone described himself simply as a businessman, but he had heard that the man was responsible for the Achilles Irrigating Canal outside Plains and that he was also building up Two Forks, in the eastern part of the county, and another area named Farley, just west of Two Forks.

And he knew the man dealt with cattle, railroads, and land. Was it something to do with Curfew Bakertone and his "business" that had driven Hank Sayles to write? Clint had a hunch, and mostly he believed in his hunches. It was a question of listening carefully, after all.

Again he caught Bakertone's sinewy glance coming over to his table. And he had the sudden impulse to walk over and say hello, for obviously the man was curious, and it was in the Gunsmith's nature to be open with people; unless, of course, the action dictated otherwise. In this case, he thought it might save a lot of time just to let a man like Bakertone know he was in town, that he was minding his own business, and that if he—Bakertone— had anything on his mind, just say it. Clint had to laugh at himself at that. Getting raspy in my old age, he told himself with a wry smile. For he did have the strong feeling now that Hank Sayles's "trouble" had to do with the tight-skinned old miser at the table down at the far end of the room.

In any event, even if he had decided to get up and walk over and challenge the man, it was too late, for at that moment he saw the figure standing just on the other side of the opened doorway into the dining room. It was Hank, and he was signaling him to come.

Quickly, Clint cut his eye to the Bakertone table, but nobody appeared to be watching. He had already decided not to go over there anyway. And now he picked up his paper, signaled the waiter for his check, and waited casually as though he had all the time in the world. Meanwhile, Hank had disappeared, but Clint knew he just didn't want to wait in the doorway—since he hadn't walked into the dining room for obvious reasons—and so was probably in the lobby or possibly up in his room.

The lobby was empty, but the desk clerk had a sealed note for him.

"Someone handed you this?" Clint asked.

"They left it for you, sir. Your name is on it." He was a young man with dirty white shirtcuffs but very clean hands.

"I am saying, did the person actually hand you the note, or was it put here on your desk when you might have been away?"

The young man was flustered by the Gunsmith's direct approach. "I did step away for a moment, mister. And when I got back . . . " He didn't finish the sentence.

"Good enough."

The note simply told him that Hank would see him at the Ever & Always. It was obvious to Clint that the presence of Curfew Bakertone and his party had driven him off. But why the saloon, which was even more public, and where a man like Bakertone would surely have spies? That message was clearly for anyone else who might read the note; not for himself.

It was clear enough, then, just where Hank Sayles planned to meet him. The message couldn't have been more explicit for the Gunsmith.

As he mounted the stairs, he did not relax his attention for an instant. It wasn't until he was inside his room and facing Hank Sayles that he let go.

"Nobody saw you?" Clint asked.

"I waited till the desk boy was away. Though it was more luck than planning. I figured sooner or later he'd have to take a leak; but if he hadn't, I'd have figured another way."

"It's that tight?"

Hank Sayles nodded his thick head of red hair and red beard. "I am one happy man to see you, Clint. Didn't know for sure that you'd get my message. Or even that you'd be able to come by."

"You were able to help me out one time," the Gunsmith said. "Though I do believe I'd have come anyway, even if I wasn't in your debt. Always liked the cut of your leather, Hank."

And they stood there for a short moment, grinning at each other and fleetingly at the past that they had long ago shared down in old Ringley town.

"Well, you know what's going on good as I do," Hank Sayles was saying as they sat in Clint's room at the K.C. House. "And I just didn't feel like letting Bakertone see us together. He'll know soon enough you're here in connection to me."

"Sure enough." Clint was sitting on the edge of his bed, while his friend took the one chair, sitting in it backward, with his arms crossed on the high straight back as he faced his friend.

"Everybody sees how the immigration tide is flowing all over the short-grass prairie all the way to Colorado and yonder."

"Sure do." Clint nodded. "The land promoters have pumped this thing way the hell up and gone out of any good sense. It is vicious what's happening."

"It's hard to believe," Hank went on. "They're saying that any quarter section of land—160 acres—represents a farm with the most fertile farmland on this continent. So everybody that comes over here from Europe is bugled into becoming a farmer on land that can't support them no matter what happens."

"So what can you do about it?" Clint asked mildly. He was as outraged as Sayles, but he knew anger didn't help the situation. The cynical land promoters with their insidious campaigns all over the country—especially back East—and in many European countries besides were running wild with success.

"But do you know the latest?" Hank asked, pushing his Stetson further back on his head. He was a big man, with a thick girth, but there was no extra fat on him. His face was round, reminding Clint of a child who grinned easily. As, indeed, Hank Sayles was like a child in many ways. He was a happy addition to any group. And Clint knew, too, that he was a top-rated land surveyor.

"The very latest?" Clint grinned. "No, probably not."

"You know about these campaigns for the county seat?"

"I've heard about them, but what's special?"

"They often get started by speculators who throw up a few pine-board shacks and spend some money to make their 'town' the county seat."

"I've heard of it," Clint said.

"It's more than you've heard, I'm sure," Hank insisted. "Do you know that one of these speculators might engage in five, maybe six or seven of these promotions at the same time? And if he makes just one of them a county seat, he'll be well off for the rest of his life?"

Clint nodded. "Sure, I guess that is so. Somebody was bound to figure out an easier way."

"It's simple out here," Hank said. "You buy the land, see, and if your spot is made a county seat, all you do then is sell to the immigrants at a good profit whatever you'd bought for the price of a bag of marbles."

Clint was nodding. "I'm getting your drift. What you're leading up to is that it's getting worse."

"A lot worse."

"Hunh."

"Clint, I find it hard to answer the question why men whom I know to be decent, home-abiding citizens can resort to bribery, gunplay, even murder, just in order to gain the distinction of having helped make their town a county seat. I mean, there are feuds!"

"I have been hearing it," Clint said, nodding his head slowly. "Kansas in particular seems to be seething with it. But tell me what Curfew Bakertone is doing in Plains."

"That's not an easy one," Hank replied. "Though I'll bet Mr. Bakertone is here dealing. You know he built the canal, and he's got his finger in God knows how many pies."

"So it's Bakertone being here that brought you to write me."

Hank Sayles was nodding even before Clint had finished his sentence.

They fell silent for a long moment, while Hank built a cigarette and Clint followed suit; each had his own thoughts, yet Clint could feel the closeness of being together with the same question.

Presently, Clint said, "You're still surveying, I take it from the sign outside your office."

Hank nodded. Lighting his cigarette, he stubbed the burnt sulphur off the wooden lucifer with his thumb.

"And you've called on me to help you." Clint finished rolling his smoke and lit it with a wooden match he took from his hatband.

Hank nodded.

"And so we both have got to the same question; or maybe let's say I have caught up with you."

Hank Sayles's grin was rueful. And for a while neither spoke; they only sat there together, smoking and turning it all over in their minds: the question that arose from all that Hank Sayles had described to his friend the Gunsmith, and from what Clint had been feeling in the atmosphere of the town almost from the moment he'd arrived.

What was a big man like Curfew Bakertone really doing in a dinky town like Plains?

Chapter Three

The winter had been a hard one that year, and spring
had come late to the country, but now summer had
brought life once again to the land. The grass all through
Horseshoe Valley was over four inches tall, and the feed
was good. Asa Slade had even said the grazing was good.
Asa was not a man to look too easily on the bright side of
things, and when he did, it had to be bonanza time.

Like now. This day there had been nothing in the sky
but the deep, dazzling blue and the astonishing sun. That
sun was "hotter'n the hinges," as one old-timer put it. It
touched everywhere, painting its way into all the corners
of the busy little town, heating backs and hands, burning
a man's sight as it darkened his wrists, his neck, built the
great ring of sweat in his crotch, his armpits, and around
his soaking hatband. Out here on the plains, where a town
more often than not resembled pieces dropped at random, with nothing surrounding it but distance, time, and
weather, a man could wonder, if he'd a mind to, wonder

what he was doing in such a place.

On the other hand, such wonderers were few. For there was plenty to do. The land had to be conquered, as indeed the natives had been; conquered, subdued, and bent to the service of Progress.

Neither Plains nor Mile Butte had been an exception to this edict of destiny, sent, it was supposed, from on high. At any rate, it happened to be the guiding light, the binding force, this hardly articulated belief that nature and lesser men and women would indeed bend to the superior force of this new era that had sprung with the final joining of the two great oceans, joining across the huge continent, via the railroad and the will of Manifest Destiny.

No one, however, could say it better than Asa Slade. Not even such an articulate individual as Curfew Bakertone, who took a number of paragraphs to extol the riches that lay in the Great West, just waiting for the brilliant brain, the loving hand, and the lawful embrace of man to take and make use of.

Asa, uneducated, hardly able to write his own name, put it in simple, frontier poetry.

"Them what has, gits. You keep yer powder dry, yer nose clean and yer pecker ready, and each time you go yerself one better."

And in point of fact, the seventy-year-old curmudgeon had accomplished just that, riding his thirty-year-old cook and housekeeper to the point where the bed had crashed to the floor and he had not missed a stroke—nor had she—as together they pounded deliriously to the best climax either could remember in their ten-year relationship.

They lay now on the horsehair mattress—the sheets having disappeared some time before during the fury of their passion—sighing, wet with perspiration, their breathing now in perfect unison as the delicious aftermath stole through every grain of their delighted bodies.

They slept.

"I could use me some more," Asa said, awakening quickly, like he always did, being bred to the frontier. "Exceptin' how about rustling up some Arbuckle first."

Dorothy, his companion—whom he called Honeydew—yawned and stretched, twisting her voluptuous body so that her right breast with its large nipple brushed against her companion's face, lightly as breath, and the next thing she knew he had that nipple in his mouth and was slowly sucking.

"Thought you wanted coffee," she murmured, having a hard time speaking as waves thrilled through her aroused body.

"Ain't no way I can get coffee and tit in my mouth at the same time," he mumbled.

"I want to be on top this time," she said, throwing her leg across him and lifting herself up to let his rigid member slide into her flowing orifice.

"Jesus . . . " He breathed the word in exquisite gratitude for this moment in his life.

And as they worked into their single rhythm, so easily, so knowing each other through the delight they had long shared, Honeydew felt the tears stinging her eyes; and Asa, his whanger hard as the handle of a pitchfork, probed hard, deep, and in perfect rhythmn with her as they moved faster and faster and came in the ultimate moment.

"Better than ever," Asa murmured.

And as she looked down at him, lying beneath her with his eyes closed in sleep, she thought how much he looked like a young boy.

Asa and Honeydew were spending the evening in town, this time in Mile Butte, at the Forty Hotel. Asa, as he put it to himself, admired to stay over in town every once in a while. And he generally brought Honeydew with him. Being his cook out at the outfit when he wasn't about didn't make much sense, since he wasn't sampling her victuals anyhow. And he liked taking her to town, sometimes to Mile Butte, sometimes to Plains. A kind of holiday, it was. With dinner in the restaurant and a different bed to have fun in. It was like a party, and he liked watching her enjoy it.

This night, though, he had to leave her for a while. It was business, he explained.

And so here he was, in a back room of the O.K. Saloon, seated at a round baize-topped table with his stubby fingers wrapped loosely around his glass of whiskey, which he had just lowered. His eyes were on the stringy, cadaverous-looking man on the other side of the table. Curfew Bakertone was always a cleanshaven man, with his skin stretched so tightly over his face and hands that he seemed to shine in a strange way. A clever Boston newspaperman some years earlier had written that Mr. Bakertone looked as though his skin was too tight for him, like an ill-fitting suit of clothes. The newswriter abruptly found himself looking for work after that noteworthy attempt at creative description.

"The point is, Slade, that I can arrange for either Plains

or Mile Butte to become a shipping center. Of course, in either case, since they're not that far apart, it isn't really so important. Except from a certain point of view," he added quickly, throwing up a long thin hand as Asa Slade started to speak. "I haven't finished," he went on.

He paused to reach for his glass, his cold eyes hard on the rancher, who had taken out tobacco and papers.

"We are both well aware, Slade, of the competition between Plains and Mile Butte for the county seat of Bullock County and, uh, all the difficulties that entails." He put down his glass, then, holding it loosely at its base, moved it about slowly on the baize tabletop as he continued. "I want to know where you stand in this situation."

"I don't give a shit who's got his ass on the county seat, Bakertone. All I am interested in is stopping the goddamn rustling, owlhooting, and thieving of horses and cattle that's bin going on."

"I understand. But you see the way things are now. There isn't much in the way of the law."

"There ain't nothin'," snapped Asa. "There never has bin, not since I bin knee high to a prairie dog. That's the way this country has bin. Oh, there's been some good lawmen, I know. But a man won't go broke countin' 'em on one hand. Take that piss-poor Studley . . . "

Something that sounded to Asa Slade like a chuckle came out of the other man's stringy throat, while his Adam's apple pumped up and down a couple of times. "Agreed. But you know he is without deputies, and he's an old-timer—I mean, he isn't young any more. I've contacted the authorities, trying to get a good lawman. But you can't expect someone like yourself, a man who built this country . . . "

Asa focused his cold blue eyes directly on Mr. Curfew Bakertone. "We none of us built it with bullshit, mister," he said, his tone even as a fistful of aces.

Bakertone took it with another chuckle. Indeed, the chuckle threatened to turn into a cough, but he controlled it.

Pausing for a swallow of whiskey, he sighed and then said, with his eyes looking directly at Slade's forehead, right where his eyebrows came together, "I am prepared to back the law in both towns, and I have arranged that the governor will call an election; soon, at the appropriate time."

"Election?"

"So people can vote for the county seat, Plains or Mile Butte. You might not think it important, but it is." He leaned forward suddenly, leaning on his elbows, which stuck into the table like a pair of pointed sticks. "Uh, you are not unmindful of the fact that you owe the Plains Bank rather a hefty remuneration for their services."

"If you're sayin' in English that I owe the bank, then I got to say who the hell doesn't!" And Asa glared furiously at the skinny buzzard seated on the other side of the table. "Who the hell don't owe?" he repeated, his anger barely under control. "Goddammit, the banks, the railroad—they all of them get help from the government, from Washington and all. But the cattlemen, the stockmen, they don't get nothin' but the shitty end of the stick, by God!"

"That is for certain," Curfew Bakertone put in swiftly, his words greased with possibilities.

Asa Slade was eyeing him carefully. "So what are you sayin' to me, Bakertone?"

"I am saying that we might work something out."

"I am telling you, Bakertone, I ain't for sale."

"I believe every man has his price, Slade."

"Not me!" And he pushed back his chair.

Curfew Bakertone was already holding up a restraining hand, his taut face wrinkled in a plea for understanding. "Of course, Slade. Of course. Do wait. Hear me out. You see, I know your kind. You have built the West, as I mentioned earlier. You stockmen, the so-to-say second generation of pioneers, you have built this country, carried the spirit of our Great Land into all the corners. In a word, you have built America! And I can do no more than take off my hat to you. You and your brothers-in-arms, in the discovery and creation of a Great World for all our children. There is no question there. None whatever! But . . . "

His index finger rose like a great spike in front of him. "But you have suffered the slings and arrows of the elements! The Great Die-up, to name but one disaster, when all your cattle froze all over the West, and the results of that catastrophe are still being suffered. I know. I know! I know full well your feeling. And you, of course, must not lose your herd, your land, your home—the home you carved out of the wilderness!"

"And I damn well ain't going to!" snarled Asa Slade, and he stood up and started to the door.

"But you will, Asa, you will."

Those words, spoken so softly, and especially the use of his first name, stopped the cattleman in his tracks.

He turned and looked squarely at the man who was still seated and quite at his ease, with his long, thin, rusty fingers lying on the green baize like a pair of spiders.

"I am not for sale, mister, and you had for sure better know that."

"As I've already said, every man has his price."

"Not me, by God!" And he turned back to the door.

Curfew Bakertone's words, issuing out of that stringy throat, from that cavernous body hidden in that dead-black suit, cut into the room with the ease of a razor slicing a fresh apple.

"Oh, but you do, Mr. Slade. You do. Otherwise, why did you accept my invitation to come and see me?"

Clint Adams's first meeting with Tony Miller had been a huge surprise: that moment when she'd come riding along on the little blue roan and he had suddenly been staggered by the beauty with the chestnut hair and soft, doelike brown eyes. In the days following he had thought of her and their time over many mugs of coffee out at her ranch. And he had been thinking of riding out to see her again. He had the pretext of her difficulties with Asa Slade's ZT outfit; anyway, he was concerned about her welfare. Butch Holmes and his boys were surely looking like trouble. Plus . . . plus he just wanted to see her. Which was the main reason.

His surprise was even greater than the first time when, stepping out of the K.C. House, he saw the little roan at the hitching rail. But the girl was nowhere in sight, so he stepped over and took a closer look at the roan.

She must have just ridden in, for he could see that the horse was warm from a recent ride. But where could she be? The coffee shop, the restaurant? He had almost made the mistake of avoiding the house restaurant in favor of a cafe down the street. And sure enough, there she was, seated alone at a table down at the far end of the room.

He figured she must have already seen him, for she turned as he approached, smiling up at him. "I saw you through the window. I was hoping you'd come in."

"May I join you?"

"But of course. Please sit."

"Are you in the hotel here?" he asked, still in his surprise at running into her. Not to mention his great pleasure.

"I'm having trouble getting a room. They're filled up."

"Oh, they've got to find something," he said.

"I'm not worried. I've come in to get some needed things. Although I wasn't happy leaving the ranch just like that. I may go right back and not stay."

"Your brother handling it?"

"Andy and Mr. Weller. His outfit borders on ours."

"I was thinking of coming out to visit you," Clint said.

"That would be nice." She smiled suddenly and then dropped her eyes, and he noticed the slight color in her cheeks.

"Have you had any more visits from the ZT boys? You know, it's not really my business, but you should have someone there with you."

She said nothing to that. The waitress came, and he ordered coffee.

Then, looking at him, she said, "You know, there's something funny going on, something strange."

"What do you mean?"

"You know those men that came, that one who said he was the ZT foreman and those other two?"

"What about them? They didn't ring true to you?"

She stared at him in complete surprise. "You mean you felt that that too?"

He nodded. "I had the definite feeling that that fellow calling himself Butch Holmes wasn't any foreman. Not for a man who runs a big outfit like the ZT."

"But . . . but what . . . " She was looking at him in bewilderment. "What is it?"

"I don't know. I am not saying that they weren't part of the ZT outfit. But I doubt very much that their boss knew they were doing what they were doing."

"Do you mean riding over to our outfit, or the branding?"

"Either or both."

"Phew!" And suddenly she looked like a schoolgirl as she said that expression.

He smiled at her, feeling her softness in himself now. "I'd like to ride out to the crossing and take a look around. I mean, if that's all right with you."

"Oh yes—oh yes, it's all right!" And she was smiling broadly at him now. And then all at once her frown returned. "Do you think those men were doing something without Asa Slade knowing about it, then?"

"I wouldn't be surprised. But that's just why I want to take a look around out there. I might even ride over for a visit to the ZT."

"But not on my account, Mister . . . I mean, Clint. I don't want you to go to trouble on my account."

"I'll keep that in mind, miss."

"Tony."

"Miss Tony." He stood up. They were both laughing.

"When will you ride out to the ZT?"

"When will you be done with your shopping?"

"Pretty directly, I'd say."

"That's when I could be riding out to the ZT. I can go by your place at the same time, if you like."

"Or we could both head straight for the ZT. I don't need to stop over in town tonight."

He cut his eye quickly at her then, but she simply looked back at him.

"Good enough," he said.

"Good enough!" she repeated, holding back her laughter until he made a face at her, and then they both laughed. As they left the dining room, he wanted like mad to put his arm around her. But he didn't. After all, he had learned early in his life that the best things need to take place in their own time.

Curfew Bakertone enjoyed the hospitality of any number of establishments both in Mile Butte and Plains, as well as, of course, a number of other towns in the West. Since his "office"—aside from his headquarters in Boston—was in his head and in the tiny yet precise jottings that he maintained on the backs of various envelopes that he kept in his coat pocket, he was able to work at any place and at any time. Just as it suited him.

At the present moment, he was seated in an upstairs room at Mile Butte's Better Pastime Saloon and Gaming Emporium across a table from Harvey Whent, who had just arrived. He had been playing a game of solitaire when Harvey got there, and he continued to play until his hand was finished, while Harvey waited in careful silence.

All at once the game was concluded, and Curfew dropped his cards onto the table.

"I always win," he said with a sigh, as though he'd been cursed. Although it was quite evident to his guest that he had lost.

Mr. Bakertone sat back in his chair, his rail-thin body not disturbing the squeaky furniture at all; it didn't make a sound. Sometimes the man was like a shadow, Harvey was thinking. It almost seemed he didn't even breathe. Harvey tried a smile, though he didn't feel at all like smiling.

"I understand your auction was a big success, Harvey."

"Well, let's say it was successful," Harvey said, with a smaller, more careful smile this time.

"A big success," Curfew Bakertone said, as though the other hadn't spoken. "Studley says it was a big one."

He had been looking steadily at Harvey as he spoke, and now he continued to do so, his eyes seeming to glow; at least so the man across from him thought.

"I do not appreciate your efforts at hiding, Harvey. I had thought you understood that."

"But I do. I certainly do!"

"After all, let us not forget that the operation was wholly my idea."

Harvey knew that, of course, it wasn't, since the idea had been his, only he held his tongue, swallowing.

"And I do expect openness, honesty from my, uh, associates," Curfew continued.

Yet Harvey Whent was no coward. He was a man who understood the role of prudence in dealing with a person of Bakertone's caliber. But he also understood that to back down too often and too easily invited disaster. Harvey Whent, honed to his calling on the riverboats, in the mining camps, the end-of-track hell-on-wheels towns, and in the plush diversities of metropolitan bunco in Frisco, K.C., Denver, and Omaha, had learned patience. Or, as somebody or other must have been the first one to say, he knew on which side his bread was buttered. And so he waited in silent fidelity as Curfew Bakertone expanded on his theme: the theme of order and law and the need thereof in the West.

"Studley ain't worth a wet fart, far as keeping law and order," Bakertone said, lapsing into "western talk," as he sometimes did in order to be "one of the boys."

Harvey Whent, keened to a razor edge, listened to the real talk, which was between the words, as Curfew Bakertone continued.

"But Studley does have a backing. People like him. He is a man who has got his uses. He knows both towns. Knows the people, the pigeons and the skunks." He paused, eyeing Harvey carefully to read his reaction. Harvey was a tomb.

"I want you to bring your next shipment to Mile Butte," Curfew said, and he saw Harvey's left eyelid twitch. Scored there, by God.

"Is that wise? I had trouble with Studley already in Plains, like I told you. He may be loyal to you, Bakertone, but he can cut me down with that easy gun of his just on account he don't like the way I sniff."

"Just be careful with him, that's all. I don't want him—or anybody!—to know that you are connected to myself. You understand?"

"I understood the first time you told me, ten times back," Harvey said, suddenly enjoying his impatience as it found relief in his testy reply.

Curfew Bakertone handled this little spat of rebellion by rolling his icy glance down the full length of his nose into the spot where there was a wild hair sticking up between Harvey Whent's eyebrows.

Harvey held his ground, even though it took his best effort.

"That will be all." And, dropping his eyes to the back of the envelope with his scribbled notes, just for an instant, Curfew reached for his playing cards, built a deck, and began to shuffle as his visitor started to leave the room.

As Harvey's hand touched the doorknob, the man at the table spoke, without looking up from his cards.

"Harvey, have you not forgotten something?"

There was a big grin on Harvey Whent's small face as he turned back into the room, his hand not leaving the doorknob. His tone was casual.

"I was letting it be a surprise, Curfew."

Curfew Bakertone pursed his lips, his eyes smiling at his cards, and, still without looking up, said, "I hope I shall not be disappointed, Harvey."

Harvey gave a little laugh. "I guarantee that your pleasure will be doubled," he said softly. And, satisfied that he had made a point, he walked briskly through the door, closing it neatly behind him.

It was really summer now, and the heat burned into the land, into the faces and hands of the cattlemen, through the shirts and trouserlegs of the horsemen, cooking the saddle horns and pommels, sweating the horses, though not the dogs, who, thickly furred, panted out the heat through their mouths and lolling tongues. As the men worked the small herd, the smell of horse urine was strong in the air, and the laconic cursing that rose now and again seemed to go nowhere.

The men worked hard, roping, busting the calves, branding, cutting the ears, and castrating. Then they released each calf, who, bawling, returned to the churning wall of beef to look for its mother. The noise, the dust, the heat, and the stench not only of urine but of men and beasts held an excitement, a power within its particular container that always gave the Gunsmith a good feeling whenever he watched a working gather.

"Do you think there are some of your beeves in that bunch?" he asked the girl on the little blue roan.

"I wouldn't be surprised, though I really don't know," Tony said, and she let out a sigh.

They had ridden out from town, aiming to reach her place around the middle of the afternoon, but, seeing the cloud of dust, they had ridden over to take a look. And they'd come upon a scene just like the one Clint had ridden onto not long before on his way to Plains.

"They ZT men?" he asked her as they rode closer.

"I'd bet on it." Then, after a moment, she said, "Yes, there's the foreman, Hank Billings." She nodded toward a man on a big white stud horse cantering toward them.

The man on the stallion had all the looks of a foreman, but he was certainly not the beefy bully who had ridden into the Miller outfit with his pair of gunslingers just recently.

Drawing rein, the big man didn't smile. But his manner

of speaking was as direct as his look at the girl and the Gunsmith.

"Miss Miller, if you're looking for Double M calves, you won't find any here."

"I think I'll be the judge of that, Mr. Billings."

"Go right ahead." Billings cut a hard eye at Clint. "Take your friend along with you." And he started to turn the big white horse.

"Mr. Billings."

Clint was surprised by the steel that suddenly appeared in Tony Miller's voice.

The foreman drew rein, and while his horse fussed at some deer flies and bobbed his head, his bridle clinking, he canted his head toward the girl. "What you got on your mind, miss? You still claiming there's brand-switching going on? Take a look!"

Clint was impressed by the girl's not backing down an inch.

"I want to know who that ruffian was that rode over to the MM last week and claimed he was foreman of the ZT."

"Did he have a name?"

"Butch Holmes."

"Oh, yeah." Billings looked away then, squinting into the sunlight. "Him. See, we got two, three foremen on a big outfit like this here. What'd he do? I know him. Sometimes he talks a bit rough."

"He didn't talk rough," Clint said, suddenly cutting in. "He was boozed, and so were his friends. I sent them packing."

Suddenly Hank Billings was noticing the man on the big black gelding. "And who are you, mister?"

Clint cut his eye quickly at Tony to see how she was taking the ZT foreman's tone of voice.

Then he said, "You might figure me to be a kind of foreman over at the MM." Out of the side of his eye, he saw the girl start a smile but then stop it. He had all his attention on Hank Billings, bristling now.

"What you mean, kind of foreman? What's that?" The sneer was almost like a slap.

"It means, if you or any of your boys mess with MM beef you'll answer to me. That's exactly what it means." He leaned forward just a little, so that he was freer in the saddle. "You understand me, do you?"

The foreman started to say something, but he cut it off, taking a second careful look at the Gunsmith. Then, not saying anything, working the chew which he'd been carrying in his wide mouth, he turned the big stud horse and rode back to where his men were working.

"I hope you didn't mind my saying that," Clint said.

"I wanted to cheer!" Her eyes were shining as he looked at her.

"I said that to turn him off and to get you some time to see what we can think of. What line to take with them."

They had turned their horses and were cantering across the carpet of rusty-colored buffalo grass.

Later, when they stopped at a creek for water, she said, "Would you like to be the MM's foreman? I mean, like for a couple of days? That's about all I could afford to pay: a day, at most two. But it would be a big help."

He waited a beat, and then he said, "Sounds like a good deal, though I expect to eat hearty. That in the deal?"

"You know the deal in hiring; it includes board and food. Right?"

"Right." He nodded, squinting at the sun, which was a good halfway down to the horizon. "We ought to make it back to your place well before nightfall."

"I think it'll be sooner than that," she said. "I'm not all that far."

"I know, but I am allowing for extra time," Clint said. He had walked Duke out of the creek, where he'd been letting the water play on his legs, and now he drew rein.

"Extra time? What for?"

"For our shaking those two riders who are following after us," Clint said. And then he wondered instantly if the girl had thought he was thinking of time for something else.

Chapter Four

She was wearing a cocoa-colored blouse, black riding breeches, and a yellow silk scarf around her neck; her dark, chestnut hair fell to her shoulders, and one long, curling wave had slipped forward and lay on her breast. Her cheeks were flushed as they sat looking at each other over the kitchen table, where they had just finished supper.

Through the window the last daylight came, touching the side of her face, and Clint Adams felt something catch inside him at her beauty. It was a beauty that was very quiet—not external, but the kind that shone through from something very deep inside. At the same time he found her nose to be exquisite, but then, going to her other parts, he was unable to decide which were outstanding. Her eyes, her brow, the tips of her earlobes, her full mouth, and her unbelievable figure; he was totally unable to name what was "the best." In any case, he knew full well that it was the totality of the separate externals, plus

that special something inside that was inhabiting her—
the force that moved her, brought her smile or frown, her
way, her manner—that brought his heart to its present
pounding and his erection to a rigidity that would surely
rip his pants if nothing were done about it.

"I hope you had enough to eat," she said.

"It was great," he said, trying to ease himself on his
chair.

"Are you all right? Is anything the matter?" She had
gotten up and was reaching over for his plate, with her
right breast almost brushing him. He thought he would
lose his mind.

And then the next thing he knew he was standing facing
her, taking the plate out of her hand and putting it on the
table, while they were both swept into each other's eyes.

Then, without a word, feeling her breath on his face,
he put his hands on her shoulders and drew her to him.

Her kiss was soft, fresh as dew; her two hands, holding
his arms, were like her kiss—giving, but not in any way
taking.

"I think we had better lie down," he said, speaking
through her chestnut hair into her ear. And, taking her
hand, he led her into her bedroom.

"Please hook the door," she said. "Andy could come
back sooner. Though he said he'd stay over awhile."

He was already unbuttoning her, trying not to go too
quickly, savoring each button, each touch, each breath
on the side of his face as she helped him.

It seemed an age, and yet neither rushed; then they
were both naked. He laid her down on top of the bed
clothes and slipped down beside her, his erection up firmly between her thighs. And then they began exploring

each other with their hands, while he began probing lightly with his rigid organ into her already wet bush and slippery lips, his hands playing over her buttocks, which had
begun to undulate. She had reached down to his behind,
holding it as he stroked his member inside her thighs,
though without entering her. Her hand then moved to
his balls, reaching around between her own spread legs
and just making it. At the feel of her fingers he thought
he would shoot everything right then and there. But he
held.

Now he moved her onto her back, her legs spreading
as he rose up on his elbows and knees, and with her
stroking fist she guided him inside.

She was very wet, tight, exquisitely so, with total
acceptance in the delicious grip of her vagina. Undulating
slowly, they worked their bodies from their initial sepa-
rateness into one thrusting, rutting rhythm of total delight;
faster, and then faster still, yet with no rushing, no hur-
rying, knowing that they had all the time they needed. And
they took it—every second of it, every last exquisite drop,
as he rode her high and low, slow and fast, alternating to
extract the most incredible joy either of them could ever
have imagined. They moved faster now, their bodies all
but flailing each other, bucking and fucking to the very
ultimate impossibility that their thrashing flesh could just
barely stand.

They collapsed from the paradise of their pounding
passion into the paradise of their exquisite satiation.

The Ever & Always Best Saloon lay somnolent in
the muggy afternoon silence. A lone forty-and-found
cow waddie stood at one end of the long bar, his lean,

leathery frame bent toward a tumbler of trail whiskey; there were two men playing checkers at one of the green baize-top tables. A low though thick cloud of cigar smoke lay almost halfway down from the ceiling of the almost airless room. Two rheumy-eyed old men with grizzled limbs were seated separately in the row of wooden chairs that lined the long back wall that faced the bar. Their thoughts, by the look of them, had to be on the past. For sure, there was nothing in the Ever & Always at that time to be interested in. A black and white cat sat with a leg up, near the dead stove, licking his crotch.

Noble Studley was standing alone at one end of the bar, his eyes following the pear-shaped bartender—a man named O'Casey—as he polished the top of the bar. Studley, known now as the marshal of Plains—though, in actual fact, he was only the acting marshal—was studying the thick black hairs inside the bartender's pitted nose as he breathed heavily. Mr. O'Casey was a big man with most of his body in his hips, narrow-shouldered, with a sloping belly with apparently no demarcation at the point where it became a chest.

Noble Studley now watched him as he wiped, even polished the bar. Mr. O'Casey did not raise his eyes, ignoring a fat blue fly that buzzed about his fine growth of thick black hair.

Studley knew that head of hair. That had been in the early days; back, or rather up, in the Gold Hills. The big bonanza. And O'Casey and his head of hair, along with Studley's swift apprehension of the most profitable marks, had earned the two of them not a small poke.

It had been the practice to pay for everything in gold dust. And O'Casey, whose name then happened to be

Hooligan, was in the responsible position of weighing the dust as the miners checked in—for drinks, food, or gambling costs. While Studley—and for some strange reason he had kept his name—had the job of distracting the attention of the mark while Hooligan-O'Casey handled the dust. Everyone knew Hooligan to be a nervous man, always scratching or fidgeting, and very often running his fingers through his thick head of hair. But he was known for his honesty and the accuracy of his scales.

Later, of course, each night after the hard work was ended, Studley and his pal would wash the yellow dust out of that great head of hair into a pan. And now Studley, looking again at O'Casey's fine head of hair, recalled those days with fondness and nostalgia, without offering O'Casey even the slightest whisper or glance of recognition of their former amicable and profitable partnership.

Nor did the bartender reveal that he had ever before even seen the person standing there with his marshal's badge, his big six-gun, his limber hands. Suddenly, without realizing what he was doing, he found himself looking down at his own hands, at his fingernails, which in those days had grown long, so that they could accumulate and then deposit as much of the yellow wealth as possible while stroking through his luxuriant and wealthy head of hair.

"You be the new marshal?" O'Casey said conversationally, as he discovered Studley noticing his looking at his hands.

"Yup. I be the law. Acting. Actin' marshal."

"Not much difference than real," O'Casey observed sagely.

"Uh huh. There ain't."

"You catch a bullet, it ain't gonna be any the less on account of you ain't the real marshal." And the bartender chortled at his little remark.

Marshal Noble Studley, known years before as one of the fastest guns in the West, didn't crack a single line in his stony face. The man who had ranked with Dallas Stoudenmire, John Wesley Hardin, Big Jim Courtright, and the like just stood there taking it in. O'Casey was surprised to discover that he was wondering if Studley ever wondered how come he still hadn't made it to Boot Hill, like just about every gunman did, some more sooner than later. But he was not really an imaginative man, and the thought was fleeting and bore no fruit.

Noble Studley, for his part, was feeling mighty relieved that he had finally landed himself a job—even though as an acting lawman—after some months of nothing. Yet, what particularly galled him was the suspicion— really, an almost certainty—that he was over the hill. The reflexes were just not the way they used to be. He was fast, still faster than most, but he wasn't quick. That is, he didn't have that extra that put him ahead even of himself. And he knew it, and it gnawed at him. At the same time, he knew he couldn't give up. He had seen old gunslingers ending up—if not as permanent real estate— then like old bronc stompers: stove up and living in the past, with nothing to show. Not a damn thing.

And so when the job had come, he'd seized it. What the hell, it was what he knew how to do. And if he did it well or did it badly, well, that was the whole point of it, and it always had been. Hadn't it?

But the worm was there. As he saw O'Casey watching him, sizing him. As he knew others in town were also doing. Was he fast enough? Would he make it with the rough boys? And vaguely, in between such thoughts, he wondered why he'd been offered the job. Because he was a good lawman? Or because he was a has-been?

It was at this point that he heard the batwing doors smack open, and looking into the big mirror in back of the bar, he saw the two men walk in. The one had a pockmarked face, the other a broken nose. He caught them looking in his direction as they headed toward the other end of the bar.

In the mirror, Studley watched them. He knew them. They were ZT men, and he wondered why Asa Slade had hired them, though he already knew the answer to that. He truly did.

Now one of the pair, the one with the broken nose, detached himself from his companion and ambled down to where Studley was standing. The moment Noble Studley had anticipated was now at hand.

"You two boys can check your guns with the barman," he said. "New law in town, since Henderson and that other feller was kilt at the woman auction."

Curfew Bakertone was delighted. Thrilled. And it showed what you could get out of a man when you demanded the best, he told himself. For Harvey Whent had surpassed himself this time. And of course, that was due to the discipline and demand imposed upon him by his master! For the dapper little bunco man had delightfully "doubled his surprise," as, indeed, he had promised.

"It is not possible to tell you girls apart," Curfew was saying, as the one who had opened the door for him swept off her jacket, thrusting two prominent teats almost into his face as he sat down on the horsehair sofa. Her twin, meanwhile, did nothing other than simply stand where she had been standing when he'd entered the room. And yet, just standing there, she radiated something that brought an instant erection and a joy that possessed him completely.

"I'm Connie," said the one who had led him to the sofa.

"And I'm Rose, Mr. Bakertone. What can we do for you?" asked the other with a smile, as she stood before him, smoothing her palms over her hips and smiling down at him.

"How to tell you apart," he said. "That is the question."

"We each have a special birthmark," Connie said.

"May I ask where?"

"That's for us to know and you to find out, sir." Rose, seating herself on his other side, reached over and put her hand on his knee.

"Con, maybe Mr. Bakertone would like us separately."

"I hadn't thought of that," said her sister with a quick smile. And she cocked her head archly at the man seated between them, whose trousers were taut with his driving erection.

"I, I do believe I'd like to try you both," Curfew almost whispered, and he had to clear his throat.

He smiled at one, than at the other—both blond, both with blue eyes, both with marvelous lines, curves, proportions, both with that teasing, tantalizing something that drove him into the most savage excitement he'd ever experienced. By Godfrey, that damn little Whent knew how to do things, and that was a fact!

But he had no time to consider the man who had made this moment possible. His whole attention was on his two delicious companions.

"I can't make up my mind which of you to undress first," he said, managing a sort of control over his breathing so that his words came out more or less normally.

"I think we can help you," Connie said. "What do you think, Rosie?"

Rose was already slipping off her blouse, and Curfew was helping her. Her sister, meanwhile, was unbuttoning Curfew's jacket and running her fingers along his silk shirt, just in the area of his belly button.

Now Rose began to remove one of his shoes, running her hand up his leg toward his knee as she did so.

Suddenly Curfew sat up. "Ladies, you put me in a helluva mess. I mean, how the devil am I going to decide which one of you to enter first? You know that is a terrible decision for a gentleman to make."

They both laughed at that. And Connie said, "Rosie, let's make it easy for him, shall we?" She ran her hand along the inside of his thigh and finally found his rigid stick.

Fondling it, she said, "We'll make up your mind for you."

Her sister stood up and began taking off her clothes. First the top, which was a silk blouse covering her firm and very prominent breasts, both of which now bounced into Curfew's sight. Meanwhile, as his erection drove to its ultimate length and thickness, Connie began unbuttoning his trousers.

Curfew had started to take off his shirt, but, finding Rosie's delicious teats in his face, he reached up and brought one of them into his mouth. By now Connie had his cock out of his pants and was kissing it, licking it, stroking it with both hands.

He reached down and pulled off Rosie's drawers and slid his hand into her crotch.

"I dunno which way to go!" Curfew gasped in his total delight.

"We'll take care of that problem," Rosie said, thrusting her bush against his hand.

Connie mumbled something incoherent, for her mouth was filled with his quivering erection.

"Know which of us you want to give it to?" Rosie asked, rubbing her bush against his face.

But Curfew Bakertone was beyond speech, beyond decision, out of this whole world. The three of them were on the bed now, feeling, playing, sucking until he thought he would lose his mind totally. Then he entered one; he would never know which. Then he entered the other. Stroking each time, wiggling, and thrusting and squeezing. Again and again and again . . . Until the moment came when he just was not able to withdraw himself.

And they kept whispering to him, "Which one? Which?" While the endless moment squeezed every drop out of him. And he must have traveled further than madness, and he came and came and came until the last exquisite drop was spent.

But into whose orifice Curfew Bakertone deposited his final coming, he never knew. Nor did he care.

He hadn't realized that he'd fallen asleep, and he only knew his situation when he awakened to someone licking along the inside of his thigh, while someone else—or was it the same person?—began teasing his balls. And still another hand started to fondle his stirring organ.

And now they were again in tandem, kissing, licking, sucking, feeling, and fucking. And again Curfew wondered who he would favor with his coming, and again he failed. Utterly.

There was a beatific smile on his cavernous countenance as he slept, his entire body limp as the proverbial dishrag.

The two sisters, one on each side of him, raised up, each on an elbow, and looked across at the other.

"God, I hope the old buzzard doesn't want thirds. I'm pooped."

"The question is, dear sister," said Connie with a wicked smile, "the question is not whether we are pooped, but whether he is." And she reached over and patted Curfew's very limp organ.

There was no response, and so they continued to lean on an elbow, facing each other across the now sleeping body of Curfew Bakertone. Presently they grew tired and each lay down, and in another moment all three were sleeping soundly.

It was a moment that had suddenly just happened. Studley had not wanted it, had even tried not to let it build. Yet it had. Inevitably. The way those things just did. And now, as he stood there facing the man with the broken nose, with his partner watching from the other end of the bar, he felt a chill run through him.

Then he heard himself saying, "You can lay them right on the bar. Both of you. Right there." And he nodded to where a half-empty glass of beer was standing, waiting for its owner to return from the outhouse.

The room was at once still, silent, with the only sound the ticking of the big clock on the side wall.

He was in it now, and there was no backing out. But he knew—as he had always known in the past—that there came that moment when you had to make your play, show your hand, call the turn. Or you were a gone chicken. And for a second or two, he wondered if that ticking of the clock was really his own self and not the big horologe on the wall.

"I see some men packing hardware," said the man with the pockmarked face at the far end of the bar. "What you trying to pull?"

"You men are not regular residents of Plains, and so you have to dee-posit your weapons with the law. I don't believe I want to tell you again."

They were both sneering as they lay their weapons on the mahogany. "When do we get 'em back?"

"When you leave town you can pick 'em up at my office."

"What if you ain't there?" asked the man standing nearest him.

"Then you won't be able to pick them up."

It was the man with the broken nose who spoke. He turned now to look at his companion, who nodded at him.

"Mister, we just come in to give you a message, and we'll be riding right out after we finish our drinks."

"Then when you're finished, I'll give you back your guns."

Again the man with the broken nose turned, and again the man with the pockmarked face nodded, and the first man turned back to face Studley.

Suddenly he was closer. He was real close. Studley could smell his breath, could feel the wind of it as he spoke softly.

"Butch wants to see you," he said. "That's the message. And he don't like to be kept waiting."

Then, turning easily, he nodded toward the end of the bar, picked up his gun, and started out of the saloon. His friend followed, also at an easy pace, after picking up his own weapon.

Studley, his palms sticky, watched them go through the swinging doors. And he kept watching those doors flip back and forth until they were still again.

He was suddenly aware of the bartender standing right behind him, though on the sober side of the mahogany. He turned.

"Nice fellers," O'Casey said. "They remind you of anyone?"

Studley shook his head. He saw then that O'Casey had poured one on the house. "Can't say I do."

"Recollect Hymes and Donnicker?"

Suddenly the names hit a bell. "Them two what held up the Butte stage depot?"

O'Casey nodded. "An' kilt three lawmen and their hosses."

"That was the part that hit everybody."

"The hosses."

Noble Studley said nothing. His eyes were following a pack rat that had just scooted out beneath the swinging doors.

The sun was hot all over his back, and he could feel the wetness running down his spine, where it was like a trough holding the cradle of his ribs together. His toes were wet in his boots, and his saddle horn felt like a piece of fire. Big Duke began to give off a caustic odor. Clint Adams was well aware of the dribbling lines of his own sweat working down each side of his face, all the way to his chin.

He let his eyes move closely over the horizon immediately ahead, slowly, not missing anything, studying all the edges and rims of the high land ahead. There were no long riders as far as he could judge.

The sky was clear. It was a very light blue, toward the edges turning to white, and it felt as though there was just no air this day. For sure there was no wind. Only waves of heat that moved in with a monotonous regularity.

In a short while he reached the line of box elders bordering the thin creek and walked Duke into the cool water. He sat still in his stock saddle, listening. Then, crossing the rippling line of clear water, he dismounted, lay down, and drank, and then he bathed his face, his neck, his forearms. The water was ice cold.

"Let me take a look at that shoe," he said, speaking to the big black horse. He lifted Duke's left foreleg to examine the new shoe he'd nailed on the day before. It was firm. He'd done a good job. Satisfied, he let the hoof go and stepped back to again let his eyes move slowly over the horizon.

Nothing.

But then something at the side of his vision caught his attention. And he felt the alert snap through his whole body. A horse and rider, just below the horizon, under the tall rocks yonder. He knew that he was on Slade's

ZT range, so it had to be an outrider. And then he spotted another movement, off to his left. Another rider. Well, Asa Slade for sure hadn't built his cattle empire by not minding details. Likely they knew he was here, and maybe even knew who he was.

The Gunsmith didn't care. He had decided that it was time to force somebody's hand. Withdrawing now to the cover of the box elders, he ground-hitched Duke and then built a smoke. He wanted to think; possibly by going over it, he'd find what he'd been missing. Squatting, with his vision including the area where he'd seen each of the outriders, he began again with his meeting with Hank Sayles in his room at the K.C. House.

Hank had filled him in on details mighty fast. Hank had always been a man who came right to the point, not wasting time on ruminating.

"See, I was hired to do some surveying, being as that's what I do," he explained simply, leaning back in his chair and then tilting it on its two rear legs, his fingers laced in back of his big red head.

"That is what I know," Clint had said, smiling at his friend. "Question is, what did they want you to survey?"

"You guessed it." Hank's face was suddenly grim.

"The land bordering the MM, the Miller place."

Hank nodded, letting the front legs of his chair down onto the floor again and then leaning his elbows onto his knees; his two forefingers made an arch in front of his face. He said then that it was Curfew Bakertone who had wanted the job done.

"What did you find?" Clint asked next.

"Nothing."

"Not a thing?"

Hank nodded. "I didn't expect to. I knew it had to be a trick of some kind. See, it could have been a rumor of gold, or the railroad wanting to throw down a spur, or who knows. But I'd already been over that land, that whole section there between the rimrocks—the Horseshoe, it's called."

"Didn't Bakertone know that? I mean, I get the feeling he's a right smart feller and so would likely have looked it up before wasting time and money on yourself."

"He knew. He had to know."

"Then he had to be putting on a show for somebody."

"You got it."

"But for who? The town? For selling building lots? For graze? What reason? If not to take everyone's attention away from what he really wanted surveyed."

Hank was grinning. "I see you have lost none of your sharp, my friend. I am glad, because I need you badly."

"Of course, he wouldn't say any of that," Clint went on, knitting it together. "He'd play it straight and innocent with you. He wanted that strip surveyed. Then the rumor would get out. He'd see to that, for sure. And then . . . "

"And then Horseshoe becomes a target," said Hank.

"Horseshoe becomes the target," Clint repeated, feeling the words as he spoke them, feeling their weight, their sense, their meaning. "The value would shoot up, of course."

Hank was nodding. "But why just there? That's what I can't figure," he said.

"That strip still in Bullock County?" Clint asked suddenly.

"It is."

"Closer to Plains, or Mile Butte?"

"Plains. Though not by much."

"Huh." Clint looked up at a big spot that took up almost a third of the ceiling. "Huh," he said again.

"It begins to look like Bakertone is trying to throw weight on the side of Plains for county seat, is what you're saying then." Hank Sayles had started to pick his teeth with the end of a wooden lucifer.

"And of course, maybe that fact itself is a dummy," Clint said suddenly, leaning forward.

"Meaning?" Hank was squinting at him then, not quite with it. Reaching up, he lifted his Stetson by its crown and resettled it on his head. "You lost me there."

"Maybe *decoy* is a better word," Clint replied with a grin. "Meaning that not only is Bakertone's maneuver a feint, but the feint itself could be like a double feint. If you follow my drift."

Hank's frown suddenly cleared. "You're saying that there might really be something important concerning Horseshoe, but by making it look like a bunco job, Bakertone is covering his bets but good, in spades."

"Kind of involved. But the good bunco man always hides that ace right in your own pants pocket, no?"

"Yes!" Hank Sayles answered, with a loud smack of his hand on his thigh. "Where does that leave us then?"

"Nowhere we weren't before," Clint replied. "Except that we know better what a clever sonofabitch we're dealing with."

Hank grinned. "And it leaves yours truly to know what a smart whip he's got for a partner, by God!"

It was just at that point in his reflections that Clint Adams caught the dazzle of reflected sunlight on metal or glass up beneath the rimrocks directly ahead. Somebody was signaling somebody. Had it to do with him? Had he been spotted? And who was it? He knew how close he was to the Shoshones. There was a big camp, Tony had told him, at the head of the creek, probably a mile from where he was.

Was it a Shoshone scout? Or was it one of the ZT riders? Swiftly he led Duke deeper into the box elders. And waited.

It was cooler in the trees, but he was still hot under his hatband; his hands were thicker from the heat, and as he studied the land in front of him, where he could see through the trees, there was a shimmering that made it difficult to see detail.

He had been hidden in the box elders for nearly half an hour when he heard the horses. They were coming in from his left, and he figured that they would stop at the creek for water, probably close to where he was. He checked his handgun and made sure that Duke wouldn't nicker when the horses approached by holding his muzzle.

Then they were there. Three of them. He couldn't actually see them, but he could hear them. And he knew them right away: Butch Holmes and his two buddies.

Chapter Five

"I says we rush the sonofabitch!"

It was Cole Hymes speaking those harsh words, allowing his hardly controlled intensity to speak louder than either of his two companions felt necessary.

"Fer Christ sake, keep yer voice down!" snapped Butch. He glared in the direction of Cole, who was bellied down in the sparse grease grass only a few yards away.

"He can't hear nothin' of us from that distance," Cole insisted. He ran the back of his hand across his nose, which was itching.

"I could slip around from yonder," Mint Donnicker said, cutting off Butch's response to Cole, but causing him to include the second of his "lieutenants" in his anger.

"You pair of assholes don't got a brain between yez. You know that feller could cut you down—I am sayin' the both of yez—'fore either one'd clear leather! Now shut it and listen here."

They swiftly caught the note of danger in their leader's voice—that is to say, the danger for themselves.

"We'll stick with him," Butch was saying now. "Fan wide, and keep him covered. It 'pears to me he is heading for the outfit."

His companions had frozen on the spot and were waiting silently for further instructions.

Now, as their quarry led his big black gelding out of the stand of trees, they waited for a sign from Butch.

"We'll foller, like I said. Might be he is heading for the outfit." Butch repeated.

They could barely see the Gunsmith, and they could not hear him or his horse, but Butch, who was closest, signaled and they began following on foot, leading their horses.

They could only vaguely see the man ahead of them as he moved slowly along the trail, toward the opening that spilled out of the trees and onto the long, low sweep of prairie that led up to the big ranch house, an approach to the ZT that exposed any horse or rider who wished to come in as clearly as any eagle in the naked morning sky. It was, as Butch Holmes muttered to his two companions, "A helluva way to try to close in on the ZT. There ain't enough cover for a rabbit with his ears pinned back."

And so they waited, watching from the edge of the trees as their quarry rode across the wide-open stretch of buffalo grass toward the Asa Slade ranch house.

"Sure could pick him off easy," Mint Donnicker muttered sourly, as the three of them eased up to a standing position.

"You mind me now," said Butch, his voice sharp with authority as he scratched deeply into his side. He held up his hand as, standing just inside the rim of trees, they watched the slight movement of the branches where the Gunsmith had disappeared into the thick brush and out of their sight.

"We could easy pick him off," Cole said, and he cleared his nose by blowing through his thumb and forefinger, only just missing Mint.

"Watch that, goddammit!"

"Shit, I missed!" Cole chuckled. "Losin' my good aim."

"Shut up," Butch said. "We'll try to get ahead of him so's we set up a ambush."

His companions chuckled silently at that, while the hot sun bore down on them.

Hank Billings stepped down from the young buckskin, staying close to the lion-colored horse, with only the one simple movement, nothing that would spook the animal. He had broken the yearling himself, not allowing any of his other hands to go near. Buck was a jim dandy, no question about that, and Hank Billings, a man who knew horseflesh all the way from tail to withers to muzzle, wasn't about to let any of his new or even old hands get near to spoiling him. Only maybe Bill Jolly or, in a pinch, Mike Wagner were old-timers seasoned enough to satisfy the demanding foreman.

Hank had a reputation for being persnickety, especially where horseflesh was concerned, and he had taken to the little tough buckskin the minute he'd spotted him in the wild bunch roundup up on Piney Creek. He ground-hitched Buck and then, standing swing-hipped, built himself a smoke. Lighting it with the lucifer he struck on the back of his raised thigh, he flicked the match and started toward the front door of the big log house. He was wondering where Butch Holmes and his buddies were that afternoon. He'd told his "subforeman," as Asa called him, that he wanted him to take care of some fencing north of Cottonwood Creek. And he was wondering if the man was actually following orders, along with his two sidekicks. Hank Billings had no illusions about the caliber of the three men Asa had hired "as insurance."

He found the Lord and Master of the ZT in the big front room that overlooked the great stretch of prairie leading from the butte right up to the cluster of log buildings that comprised the heart of the ZT brand—the heart and lungs and guts of Asa Slade's life work, his real purpose in staying alive, and indeed, the very sinew and vibration of his long, angry life.

His knock was answered by a brusque "Come!" And when he walked in he found himself facing his employer's back. Asa Slade was standing at the big window that watched the long approach to the heart of his cattle empire—now fallen on parlous times—and indeed commanded the whole left-flank approach from the creek, the trees, the trails from anywhere "outside" the strange fastness built and held together all those years by the leathery man with the scraggly-haired jaw like an angry bull and the hands that looked like talons.

"Like a word, Asa," Hank Billings said, by way of introduction.

"Set." Asa turned from the window. "Bin figurin' as how you might," he said.

"It's about that feller Holmes. Butch Holmes and them two sidekicks of his'n."

"Figured," Asa said, and he came forward, hooked the leg of a chair with his foot, and pulled it forward. Then, with a sudden and unexpected belch, he sat down, facing his big, bulky foreman.

"You know I done what you told me," the foreman said. "Took the three of 'em on."

"Like a depity foreman," Asa said, working his jaws and sniffing.

"That's just the part like I don't understand," Hank said. "What the hell is a deputy foreman, and what d'you mean by it, and what the hell am I doing with three assholes who don't know their dick from a gun barrel?"

His employer grinned at that, but it was a wicked grin. "I do appreciate what you're sayin' there, and I know I might not be explainin' to you, but there ain't a helluva lot I kin say."

"Those men have got somethin' to do with Bakertone, is how I sees it," Hank said. He had large, bulbous eyes, and these he turned directly onto Asa Slade as he spoke.

"Mebbe," Asa said. "Maybe. Course, like you know, Bakertone ast me to hire them on, which I sort of had to do, being as I am in no position to argue the bank."

"Thing is, why you want that stupid sonofabitch Holmes to be an acting foreman, whatever the hell that is."

"It means he's there if anything happens to you."

"What the hell's gonna happen to me, fer Christ sake!" Hank Billings's big eyes were almost jumping out as he glared at his boss.

"I don't expect anything to happen to you, Hank. You know I count on you. How long we known each other?

Long time. Maybe ten, twelve years, thereabouts."

"That's what I know," Hank allowed grudgingly, yet still not understanding why he had to have that useless trio on his hands.

Asa Slade, on the other hand, knew very well why. He had not looked forward to this moment, but now that it was here, he didn't hesitate. "They be here, in that position," Asa said slowly, with his eyes carefully watching Hank Billings for his reaction, "on account of Mister God Damn Sonofabitch Bakertone has got me—us—by the balls, and he is starting to squeeze."

Clint Adams had spotted the party of three almost at the same moment that they had stumbled upon him. He had not seen their faces, yet he was close to certain they were the same trio he had braced at the MM ranch, when he'd visited with Tony Miller.

He had simply followed an old Indian trick he'd learned years before from the Kiowa. He let them follow him, careful that they found enough difficulty to be sure he hadn't spotted their game. Winding through the brush and heading toward the big butte that he knew was the southern boundary point of the ZT, he knew the three were following him much too closely, thus revealing their inexperience. He was looking for the best place where he would pull off his ambush; finally he saw it.

They had rounded the butte, coming onto a creek, and he spotted the pencil of smoke in the middle distance, indicating that a house or cabin was ahead. Suddenly he steered Duke off the trail and walked him up the creek for several yards, stepping right out into the center of the stream. Then, instead of crossing the creek, he came back onto the bank he had just left, only several yards upstream. Swiftly, he cut back through the trees, so that he ended up shortly behind the trio.

He could hear them before he saw them. They had stopped at the bank of the creek and were conversing angrily over which way to go.

"Sonofabitch pulled the old Injun trick of walkin' his hoss in the water," someone was saying.

"Jesus!" It was the heavy man speaking, the one named Butch. "How'n hell you figger that, by God!"

"How the Injuns does it, I bin tolt," said the first voice.

"Shut up!"

"Do you reckon he's headin' for the ZT?" another voice broke in.

"Be pretty dumb if I didn't," replied the first man. "Shit, we could spend a lot of time finding him again."

"Can't tell whether he headed up- or downstream."

"D'you reckon he knows we was followin'?"

"How the hell would I know that, fer Christ sakes!"

"I say he is headin' for the outfit, and I wonder if the boss knows he is coming."

"Or Billings."

"Billings?"

"Yeah, Billings. The ramrod, you dumb shit."

"Shit, I thought you was ramrod, Butch."

"I am, you asshole, but so is Billings. And it is him what has been whipsawing this outfit all this time, not yours truly. Not that, by God, Butch Holmes don't know a helluva lot more about running a cattle outfit than a feller like Billings. But we be here on the payroll for special business. You mind that now, Cole, goddammit, and you too, Mint!"

All of which came across clear as spring water to Clint Adams, who was only a matter of yards away. And it was just at this point that he heard another horse approaching. It was clearly a horse with a rider.

He quickly dismounted and waited, as the horseman approached through the thick foliage. But then, at almost the point where he would become visible, he veered away. Clint acted swiftly, moving Duke toward the creek, being careful at the same time not to give away his position, either to the horse and rider or to the three men he had been following.

Then he heard one of the trio talking, but he couldn't make out what was being said; and then almost immediately, he heard them splashing through the creek. Almost instantly, the lone horseman had veered off and crossed the creek, on the Gunsmith's other flank.

Clint spurred Duke forward, not wanting to lose contact with the single rider, but he was too late. The rider had already crossed the creek when he got clear of the thick foliage, and all he could see was the man's back.

He was a big man, but he was bent forward over the pommel of his saddle and kicking his horse into a gallop. Clint wondered what had startled the rider into suddenly changing direction. What had he seen? The three, evidently, for judging by the position he'd been in, he would have had a more likely view of the three horsemen than of himself and Duke. At any rate, the rider was too far away now for Clint Adams to have even an inkling of who he might have been. And by now the three had clearly given up on trying to locate Clint and were heading toward the ZT.

•   •   •

The gather this time was in a pocket or box canyon not far from the Miller ranch, which bordered on the big Asa Slade outfit, as did a few others. Some old-timer humorist had, in fact, put it that just about the whole of Colorado bordered the Slade outfit.

Clint had followed the three ZT hands almost into the basin, where Slade's headquarters were spread out in full array, but he stopped just before breaking through a big thicket of willows and choke-cherry bushes. It would have been a perfect screen for an ambush.

Then they were in the clear, and suddenly Clint put his heels into the big gelding's sides and urged him to a fast canter. It was just then that the three saw him approaching and drew rein, spinning their horses to confront him.

"Do not draw!" the Gunsmith snapped, who already had his Winchester out of its scabbard, ready for action.

The three accepted this wise admonition and froze in their saddles, their horses high stepping a little with the excitement of the moment as the Gunsmith rode up fast and reined.

"I want to know why you were trailing me," he said, holding the Winchester one-handed, with its barrel covering the three chagrined trackers.

"We wasn't following you, mister," said Butch Holmes. "We wuz watching you on account of you are trespassing on ZT range. Now you tell us—"

But the Gunsmith cut him off fast, drawing back the hammer of the rifle with his thumb. "I asked you a question, mister. I want an answer."

"You are on Mr. Slade's range, Gunsmith. You got the draw on us, but don't get yerself sassy about it, by God!" Butch Holmes was clearly angry enough to do something foolish, and Clint realized he was acting that way for the benefit of his two companions.

"Take it slow, mister. I have come to call on Slade, and first I am taking a look at that branding party yonder. Last time I was here, you fellers had slapped some pretty sloppy brands onto MM stock. I am just wondering if you have maybe improved on your work." His grin was wicked as he raised the barrel of the Winchester just enough to bring a new look into the three pairs of eyes.

"No need to get yer ass in a uproar, Gunsmith," Butch said. "We ain't doing any more than watching Mr. Slade's property, on account of there has been a helluva lot of rustling going on hereabouts of late, and Mr. Slade ain't taking none too kindly to it. So put down your popgun and come on over and take a look."

The report from the Winchester hit the atmosphere that had been building, and the three men had to quiet their horses. Clint had aimed into the ground. There was no arguing or discussion now. The horses were skittish, and the three men were also spooked.

Clint nodded his head in the direction of the gather, not lowering the rifle. The three faces stared at him, almost in disbelief, and now the group cantered toward the pocket canyon. Clint kept the rifle at the ready, knowing that somebody would surely have realized their presence; in fact, he spotted an outrider off to their left as they came closer to the site of the branding party. And at that same moment, he was wondering who the stranger had been who had ridden up so close at the creek and then ridden off. The Gunsmith hadn't had a decent look at the man, though he had noticed that the horse he'd been riding had a loose shoe, judging by the print he'd left in the soft bank of the creek.

"All right. That'll do her," he said, drawing Duke down to a walk as they reached the entrance to the pocket canyon and were met by two horsemen.

"I'm here to take a look at your branding work," Clint said to the pair of riders who confronted them. "Name's Adams, and I am ramrodding the MM brand."

"Where is Billings?" Butch Holmes asked, glaring at the pair of outriders.

One of the men nodded in the direction of the canyon. He was a chunky man with narrow shoulders and a twitch under his right eye. His companion was thin with wide shoulders, and his shirtsleeves were rolled halfway to his elbows.

"I'll talk to Billings," the Gunsmith said.

The chunky man exchanged a glance with his companion, then both turned their horses and, at a light canter, led the way into the canyon, Clint bringing up the rear, with the Winchester covering his party of three. As they came through the walls of the box canyon, he felt, more than saw, the riders who fell in behind them. It was as he had expected. Asa Slade sure ran a tight string.

Curfew Bakertone leaned back in his chair, dropping his failed hand of solitaire onto the tabletop. He sighed, reached for his glass, and drank, all the time keeping his hard eyes on the man seated before him.

This was an elderly gent, a good bit older than he, yet sitting firmly under a shock of white hair, supported by a magnificent, snow-white, longhorn mustache and goatee. Curfew had only just met the man, who had knocked on his door, and was thinking that he just had to be a "colonel"; and by golly, he was.

He was, indeed, Colonel Corliss Witherspoon-Witherspoon, and, in fact, the man enjoyed a certain renown as one of the West's more astringent editors. Founder, publisher, and editor of the *Plains Endeavor*, the "West's Most Honest Newspaper"; self-anointed champion of Truth, Justice, Liberty; the standard-bearer in the battle against corruption by the railroads, the landgrabbers, the duplicitous and irresponsible exploiters through government of the Great Western Frontier, the Colonel had swiftly realized that the presence of such an important personage as Curfew Bakertone in this part of the country could, and more than likely did, indicate excitement.

Colonel Witherspoon-Witherspoon was not at a loss. Withdrawing a large red bandanna, he blew his nose vigorously, wiped, and returned the bandanna to its pocket.

"You will no doubt be wondering why I have knocked on your door, Mr. Bakertone."

"I presume you wish to interview me for your newspaper," Curfew replied, leaning back and lacing his fingers across his round belly. He began rotating his thumbs, which, his visitor noticed, were quite curved.

The Colonel beamed. Everyone invariably loved being interviewed. "Nothing very personal," he said. "No invasion of privacy. But you are known, Mr. Bakertone, to be a man of significant enterprise, a man of success and a champion of those who carry the banner of goodwill."

At this point there was a knock at the door, and when Bakertone called out to enter, one of the barmen from the K.C. House dining room entered with a bottle and glasses.

The Colonel's face lit up and he cleared his throat, beaming upon his host.

"I had heard of you, Mr. Bakertone, as a man of social grace, and now I see that this is indeed so. What a delight to meet a man not only of accomplished enterprise but of social responsibility!"

Curfew Bakertone's grin appeared instantly at those words, and the Colonel noted—as had other persons—how his eyeteeth each stood prominently forward, giving the suggestion of fangs. Amusing, the Colonel thought, but at the same time ringing a small bell of alarm somewhere in him. Be careful, he thought, and he felt a sudden relief that the note of caution had struck before anything untoward had taken place.

"You understand, Colonel, that the company I represent—the New England Cattle, Land & Transportation Company—is concerned deeply about the development of the West," Bakertone was saying. He had lifted his glass. "To the health of the West, sir!"

And they both drank vigorously.

"It interests me, Colonel, that you should come to see me, since I too had felt the need to speak with you. How shall I put it?" He paused, his glass in midair. "I think I can safely say that we are both men of a certain foresight, that we are each concerned with what is happening in this particular corner of our Great Nation. For, though the fate of Plains and Mile Butte may not seem important to the national newspapers, or possibly even to the Congress in Washington, you and I both know that their importance is no less vigorous in the minds of the few who care for the future of our Great Nation, the future—and, let me add too, the present—of the West. In short, we surely

see, you and I, that both Plains and Mile Butte are KEY
FIGURES; lynchpins, as it were, in the success or failure
of the West!"

"Of course," said the Colonel, cutting in on it and not
wishing to be outdone. "Of course, what is needed is not
fine words—as we both are well aware—but action. I
myself see Plains and Mile Butte as typical towns, typical
problems; that is to say, I see the need for a single county
seat, and I have said so. You've read it in my editorials,
I am sure."

Bakertone was nodding. "I have. And I am in full
accord with your view. You reveal, may I say, an objec-
tive point of view that is wholly correct for an established,
honest newspaper." He put down his glass, following a
vigorous swig, and exhaled loudly, with pleasure. "And
it is for this reason that I am happy to—may I suggest?—
join forces with you."

The Colonel was beaming all over his ruddy face.
"Although your work and interest in our part of the
world have shown themselves in fine results—the canal,
for example, and in other ways—I know in my heart of
hearts that it hasn't been easy. People, let's face it, are
sometimes slow to see what is good for them. And I, for
one, believe that you and your company have acted with
admirable restraint and, uh, good sense." He paused,
seeing that Bakertone, after all, wasn't trying to interrupt
him. "Yes, we can certainly work together for—well, for
the good of the community."

Curfew Bakertone was regarding him solemnly out of
his small eyes, which were close together and had heavy
lids. He remained silent, which was the last thing the
Colonel expected him to do. And he suddenly realized,
with something like a very slight chill running through

him, that he had only just scratched the surface with Curfew Bakertone. And this was even more strongly put to him in what came next.

"The first thing facing, let us say, the public, is the question of which town will be the county seat."

Colonel Witherspoon-Witherspoon nodded warmly. "To be sure. Yes. Hmm. That surely is the touchy point."

"Touchy?" Those couched eyelids had lifted like lizard skin as Bakertone surveyed the man seated across from him.

"Yes. Who—or which—will be the county seat," the Colonel replied.

"But Colonel, the county seat has already been decided." And Curfew Bakertone added, with an expression on his face that Witherspoon-Witherspoon took to be a smile, "Of course, there will be an election."

"Where is Billings?" Clint asked, when two more riders separated themselves from the bunched cattle and rode up. They were both staring hard at Butch and his two sidekicks.

"He ain't here right now, stranger. What can we do for you?" It was the heavyset man on the big bay horse with the wide white blaze who spoke. His companion simply looked at Clint Adams out of his pale eyes. He was a wiry-looking man, with a battered Stetson that looked as though it had been around as long as himself.

"Where is Billings?" Clint kept his eyes right on the heavyset man.

"Cal, you know where Mr. Billings is?"

"Nope," said the man with the beat-up Stetson. He was riding a dun-colored mare with a cast in her left eye.

"Then I reckon I'll go find him," Clint said, and he kneed Duke, lifting his reins slightly.

The man on the bay horse kicked his mount right in front of Duke, so that the Gunsmith had to rein in to prevent a collision.

But the Gunsmith's movement didn't stop there. In the next split second, he had taken his foot out of his stirrup and kicked the other rider in his kneecap and, at the same time, had his companion covered.

"You can show me the way now," he said, and his words were not soft.

The heavyset man on the bay horse was clutching his kneecap, his face twisted in pain, as he cursed.

"I've got your pal Cal covered while I'm at it," Clint said, raising his voice so that the men who had now ridden up could hear. "As well as Heavy, here. I am ramrodding for the MM and I have come to speak to Slade about your branding operation. I think you had better figure I am not in the mood to be messed with." He waved the Winchester. "Move it. As for you men with that iron"— he raised his voice again—"you might as well quit now, on account of you're going to have to rebrand a lot of that stuff back to the MM." His eyes were right on the heavyset man, who was still rubbing his knee. "What's your handle, mister?"

"Boone."

"Boone, you and Cal here will take me to Slade. Now let's move it."

"Thought you aimed to see Billings," Boone said.

The Gunsmith didn't say anything to that; he only drew back the hammer of his weapon. And that was louder and more clear to all present than any kind of conversation.

The sun was hot on his back as they moved away from the branding party, and it was hot on the backs of his hands, too.

At the same time he had the strange feeling as he looked over at Butch Holmes and his two sidekicks that there was something missing.

"I'm foreman here, Gunsmith. You can speak to me," Holmes said. "Mr. Slade and Billings are elsewhere."

The Winchester Clint was holding moved slightly toward the big man who was sitting his horse easy, with a big sneer on his face. "I don't reckon you'd shoot a unarmed man, Gunsmith—especially not in front of these here peaceful fellers."

Clint Adams didn't say anything to that. He kneed Duke forward and, in a moment, had drawn right up next to Holmes, who was indeed not armed, having just unbuckled his belt and handed his six-shooter to one of his buddies.

"No, I won't shoot an unarmed man, Holmes." And without the slightest warning, he lashed out with his left and slapped the big man right across the face.

The big man reeled under the force of the blow, but he stayed in his saddle.

"You see this gun, Holmes? It's harder than my fist. Now, you and Boone there can take me to Slade. I mean right now!"

Hank Billings had worked for Asa Slade more than a good while, as he on rare occasions put it to himself— rare because the foreman of the ZT was not a man to keep accounts. Like his employer, he was a man of the old breed, though a good bit junior to Asa. Since he was a button, Hank, like the old-timers, had been schooled never to ask but to find out. He was man who spoke damn seldom, but he could dress down a greener or a raunchy hand with a single look or a simple freezing of the atmosphere. Asa Slade counted on his top hand. And it could be said that his top hand counted on him. Their relationship over the years had taken on the qualities of a ritual. It was minimal, precise, and—the best of it—useful to each.

It was a surprise—almost a shock—to the big fore-man, though his expression revealed nothing, when his employer offered a drink, followed by a cigar. They'd had drinks together over the years, but not at that hour of the day, and not in Asa's office. In town, sometimes at the casual saloon meeting, and rarely.

This, then, had to be an occasion. As surely it was, since he had just braced his boss with the question of why he had those three half-assed saddlebums on his hands—Holmes, Hymes, and Donnicker, the big fat one as some-thing called "deputy foreman."

"He has got us by the short hairs," Asa said, embel-lishing on his earlier comment that Curfew Bakertone had them by the balls. "There ain't no getting around them notes at the bank, mister."

"I don't see why the buggers can't carry us," Hank said, running his forefinger under his nose where it itched suddenly. "Hell, you bin here longer than the goddamn bank, fer chrissake! You was here 'fore the town. Then these here Easterners come by an' just take over from the work everybody else already done before. I mean, like opening the country, fighting the Sioux an' Shoshones and like. I mean, shit take it!"

"I know, I know . . . " Asa was holding up his hand, his cigar clutched between two fingers. "I bin over all of it with myself and with Bakertone and, before him, Dunhower. Shit, I took Frank Dunhower for a fourteen-hand sonofabitch, but this feller makes him look like a schoolmarm."

Hank's big eyes were staring hard at Slade, thrusting with indignation. "You mean to tell me that that sonofabitch and his bank and all can just up and take your property from you! Like they can just tell you and me and the rest of the boys to roll our bedding an' git! Hit the trail!"

"They can, and that is what they be doin', by God. I mean, just about. That is the next step."

"Shit!"

"Less I come up with the mazoola."

"That is a big pile of money," Hank said, sniffing and picking up his cigar. Hank could have counted on one hand the times Asa Slade had offered him a cigar and drink like this. It was what he liked about the old buzzard: Whenever he did something, it counted.

"It is, and I ain't got it. And that, by God, is the size of it. We be jammed up tighter'n a bull's ass in fly time."

A long moment passed through the room now, as each regarded his thoughts and partook of the good whiskey and fine Havana cigar.

"Well, you know it already," Hank suddenly said, "but I got to say it anyways. I don't trust that sonofabitch Holmes an' his two buddies far as I can throw a team of hosses. Them three are trouble. So why can't we least get rid of them, since we might lose the outfit anyways? Let's do it clean." And Hank's jaw suddenly dropped when he realized how he'd been speaking to his employer. "I don't mean to be butting in on your business, but . . . "

To his astonishment, Asa Slade was grinning. And even in that gingery moment, Hank had to admit how the old boy looked pretty damn much like a wolf. For sure, he'd something up his sleeve more than arm.

"Glad to hear how you size it," Asa was saying. "Knew you'd take it like that, but I had to be sure."

"I don't read you there, boss."

"I am saying same thing as yerself. We got to git ourselves out of this here box. And we got to do it right."

Hank Billings's dropped jaw had now closed in further astonishment as his boss once again surprised him, this time with his attitude. He had always known Asa Slade to be a fighter, but this particular time, right now, it had looked like he'd come to the end of his string. But here, by God, the old buzzard was lighting up like a lucifer at midnight, all piss and vinegar. He, Hank Billings, could feel it. By God, the old man was not taking any of it lying down.

"You're askin' if I be still with you, that it?"

"No, I ain't. I by God am damn well figurin' you are with me." And Asa Slade brought his hard jaws together like a wolf snapping down on some morsel, where there was no arguing it, neither one way nor the other.

A long pause followed, while each took a drink and worked on his cigar. The pause lengthened. Hank Billings looked over at his employer as the old cattleman got to his feet and walked to the big window that faced the main approach to the ZT. Asa stood there now with his back toward his foreman, his hands hooked into his rear pockets, standing swing-hipped, like he was just any old

cow waddie waiting to cut his mount out of the cavvy
that the wrangler had just run in for the day's work.

Hank Billings took a drag on his cigar, squinting
through the smoke at the man standing in front of the
big window. He lifted his glass. Suddenly, without any
warning, he was remembering back to when he was still
wet back of his ears, not much more than a button, and
his dad and Uncle Stace were standing like Asa was right
now, standing just outside the old log barn, in the horse
corral. He'd come up on them without their knowing it,
and his dad had been talking about him, saying as how
he hoped one day to "make a hand out of the boy." And
he had felt real big then for a minute, and even some
time more. And he'd remembered that time every now
and again as he grew from a button into a man. Funny,
something like that coming into his head.

The man at the window suddenly cleared his throat,
and without turning around, he spoke.

"Rider. Down by the creek. Big black horse."

"He alone?" Hank asked.

"Just him and his horse."

"That'll be that feller Adams," Hank said. "Feller they
call the Gunsmith."

Asa Slade lifted his cigar. "That is what I know," he
said. "I bin expecting the gentleman."

The storm had ridden in halfway through the night with
a sudden sweeping wind from the north and west, slicing
sleet across the land. Then the wind slackened and the
sleet changed to a cold, drizzling rain that soaked into
everything. Close to dawn it abated, the rain drawing back
into the big dark clouds, and at last the sun came, moving

from the prairie into the little town, the land and the houses welcoming it, emitting plumes of steam as the heat met the cold and wet that was left by the passing storm.

Plains, close to the border of Indian territory, had a regular population of from twelve to fifteen hundred. The town was all wood except for the train depot, which was plastered. The sidewalks along Main Street were a good ten feet wide and made of wood. The streets were still covered with grass. Only recently, the town council had passed an ordinance prohibiting buffalo and other wild animals from running through the town's streets. To be sure, no one had seen a buffalo anywhere near the town in years; nevertheless, the council had written it thus.

There were twenty-six places in Plains where liquor was served, and a neat dozen gambling halls covered the action. Just about every device used to maintain the fine art was at hand: three-card monte, chuck-a-luck, hazard, faro, the tobacco-box game, wheels of fortune, old sledge, and, of course, poker and dice in all varieties. Each establishment that supported gambling had a bar; some had free lunch, and some offered music.

Noble Studley had decided that it had to be Plains. At least for this particular moment in his life. For, while the West was sure enough a big place, there was still a kind of communication system of arteries, like the branches and twigs and leaves of a tree that connected with everything else, and especially with the main trunk, carrying in its path all the news, the gossip, the who and where of so many of those with summer names who wished only to disappear. In brief, Noble Studley had discovered what others had also learned: that the Great American West wasn't such a great big place after all.

Yet he had somehow been drawn to Plains. He didn't know why. And when quite by accident he had run into Miles O'Casey at the Ever & Always Best Saloon he'd felt a momentary relief at seeing his old sidekick from the gold fields—O'Casey, formerly Hooligan.

And it was O'Casey who, without saying a word, had eased his old business associate in the direction of those parties who were most clamoring for law and order in Plains.

Noble Studley, being a name remembered as a premier gunfighter, and no man to argue, won the appointment easily. To his own surprise, in fact; it was a shock to Studley to discover that the reputation he had been trying to escape was exactly what now brought not only achievement but a certain respect.

Of course, it was not all honey. He had inevitably become a target. At the same time, at O'Casey's and his secret employer's suggestion—supported by certain pressure—it appeared to be a good chance for covering himself.

Hell, he could be worse off. His eyes were not good, his draw was slow; he was getting up there, by God. Besides, it didn't matter whether or not he wanted it; his new employer had made it quite clear what was expected.

Idly now, with his elbows on the bar, his back to the big mirror, Studley watched the faro dealer setting up his bank and making ready to play. He was a small man with boney arms named Chip, and he was assisted by his casekeeper, who would manipulate the small box that contained a miniature layout with four buttons running along a steel rod opposite each card. It was the casekeeper's job to move the buttons along, as on a billiard counter, while the cards were in play, so that the players could tell instantly what cards were still not dealt.

Studley continued to watch idly as the faro dealer carefully placed his layout, the suit of thirteen cards that were all spades, painted on a large square of oilcloth that had been enameled. The cards on the layout were arranged into two parallel rows, with the ace to the left of the dealer and the odd card, the seven, on his far right. There was sufficient space between the rows for bets to be placed by the players. The row closest to the players had the king, queen, and jack—which were known as the big figure— and then the ten, the nine, and the eight.

In the row nearest the dealer were the ace, deuce, and the trey—the little figure—and the four, five, and six. The six, seven, and eight were called the pot. The king, queen, ace, and deuce were called the grand square. The jack, three, four, and ten were the jack square, while the nine, eight, six, and five were the nine square.

The room had filled now; the air was thick with tobacco smoke and the smell of men as Studley watched the faro dealer shuffle and cut the cards, and then place them face upward in the dealing box, the top of which was open.

Idly watching the faro play, Studley suddenly felt someone approaching from across the room. It was a baldheaded man, with a very red dome, red face, and a thick neck.

"Studley . . . "

The voice came from behind him, and he knew it was O'Casey's warning.

"Well, if it ain't Mr. Noble Studley!" The baldheaded man was right in front of him, and a circle had instantly cleared, with the clientele crowding the walls to get out of the way of any possible lead.

And then Studley recognized Geeker. He'd shaved his head, which was why it had taken a moment. A moment in which Geeker went for the hideout inside his thick shirt.

"You're under—" Studley started to say, but he never finished his sentence, ducking and twisting his body with a sudden agility that astonished the onlookers, as Geeker's bullet smashed the big mirror behind the bar. The great sheet of glass that split out and fell, the cat that jumped screeching from where it had been sitting by the row of bottles, attracted the attention of no one. All eyes, every nerve in the room was on the suddenness of the baldheaded intruder's attack and the new marshal's nimble accuracy in dispatching that intruder to Boot Hill.

"Jeesus . . . " muttered Miles O'Casey, and the word whistled softly into the atmosphere, a mere stirring of air, not noticed by any of the stunned spectators. Yet, in a certain way, it supported the at-once-familiar tableau of angry death with, at the same time, its unique strangeness.

Noble Studley felt a totally unexpected wave of dizziness hit him, but only very briefly. He realized that he was still holding his gun. He holstered it, with the strange sense that he was not at all in charge of the situation. And then came the sudden relief, the overwhelming sweep of unique realization that he had done it. He had drawn, fired, and killed his adversary. It—something—was still there. He could only just believe it by telling himself it had happened, and by looking down at the corpse on the barroom floor.

Chapter Six

Geeker!

Studley holstered his gun, turned to the bar, and lifted his glass. O'Casey was looking at him.

"He drew on ya, Marshal. Plain as a pikestaff."

Studley acknowledged his former colleague's support by taking another drink.

"Couple men could take him down to Burt Slang's."

Studley had turned back to the room. "Get him to the undertaker," he said. "Man's been lookin' fer trouble, and by God he found it." As he put his glass back down on the bar, he realized his hand wasn't too steady.

But by God, he'd done it. And Geeker, by God, was no tenderfoot. Geeker, the sonofabitch, been on the prod ever since Leadville. Bastard with a long memory. Cut off now, it was. But it could have gone the other way. And yet . . .

Studley paused in his thought; Geeker hadn't seemed that kind of man. A sonofabitch, yes, and a man determined to be first, but there was something wrong. Because he had known Geeker well back in Leadville and around the Canton boys. And Geeker hadn't been so long on brains. He was a revengeful type, no question; nevertheless, Studley had the odd feeling suddenly that the confrontation had more to it than simply Geeker's revenge.

The room had returned to normal now as the body was carried down to Burt Slang's icehouse. Studley, leaning lightly on the bar, looked down at his hand, which was holding his glass.

"Company."

It was O'Casey's Irish accent conveying the message out of the side of his mouth. His eyes, meeting Studley's, swung toward the door at the far end of the bar.

For a few seconds Studley surveyed his old sidekick, noticing that O'Casey had a wart on the back of his hand, the hand that was moving the bar rag over the mahogany. He waited a moment, taking that amount of time to establish his independence, while he finished his drink. When he saw O'Casey look at him again, he waited just another short moment and then turned away from the bar and walked out the back door of the saloon to take a leak against the wall of the building.

Reentering the Ever & Always Best Saloon, he didn't even look in the direction of O'Casey but walked at a measured pace down the whole length of the bar till be came to the door of the back room—the room used for special card games and meetings, and to which not just anyone at all was ever admitted. Studley, even though not marshal of Plains for very long, knew very well who his host would be. After all, he may well have been slower with his physical reflexes—although Geeker certainly would not have thought so—but his wits were all with him.

All the same, he was caught in total surprise as he walked in and the soft voice seated alone at the round card table greeted him. He had indeed seen the face before, but he was not without that strange thrill and shock that hit him—all mixed up in a kind of inner confusion and excitement—which certain good-looking women called from him.

"Mr. Studley, do sit down. I am Constance Bakertone. I am so sorry you had to keep me waiting."

And Noble Studley looked into those glittering, hard, smiling green eyes and felt a chill run through him, and precisely at the same moment his manhood stirred violently in his trousers.

"I've ordered you a drink," she said, as there came a knock at the door.

It was O'Casey—formerly Hooligan from the Gold Hills—carrying two glasses and a bottle.

"Will there be anything more, ma'am?"

"No. No, there won't. And don't let anybody disturb us, bartender. Do you understand?"

Studley watched the green eyes carefully as they drilled home the point to O'Casey.

"Got'cha," said O'Casey.

When the door closed, the lady reached for the bottle, uncorked it, and began pouring into the glasses.

Studley's hand started toward his shirt pocket.

"Take a cigar," his hostess said. "In that box there." She nodded toward a box on the table near a folded copy of the *Plains Endeavor*. "I'll join you."

• • •

Now in the late afternoon, the long, slow sunlight washed across the corrals, the barn, the bunkhouse, and other outbuildings of Asa Slade's ZT spread, in that special moment that seemed to Clint Adams to be the division between the day and the beginning of twilight. It was the moment he loved best, both at evening and at dawn, when the "twilight" could be either the beginning of the day, or the end of it. It was inevitably short and, at the same time, inevitably endless. A song.

Duke was bobbing his head against the deer flies as they rode up the short stretch from the edge of the creek to the first corral. He had ditched Holmes and Boone at the creek, nodding them off as they came within sight of the ZT ranch house.

"Beat it," he'd said. "I'll locate Slade for myself." The disgust in his voice had discouraged further discussion; without a word, the two men had kneed their horses away from their escort.

But the Gunsmith had caught Butch Holmes's eye greedily on his big black gelding. His eyes were as hard as his words as he confronted the big man.

"You know what the vigilantes do to horse thieves hereabouts in the western country, Holmes?"

Holmes had gulped. "Sure enough, but what you worried about, Gunsmith? I am just admiring good horseflesh." He sat slumped in his saddle, his hand near his six-gun, a sneer on his face.

"I am not admiring the stink of what I am looking at, mister. Now git!" And the Gunsmith sat there in his stock saddle on his big black horse, with his eyes boring into the other man.

A moment had passed, and then, dropping his eyes, the big man had turned his mount and rode off with the man named Boone. The Gunsmith watched them out of sight and then proceeded on his way into the center of Asa Slade's ZT empire.

He had known he was being watched all the way in. He knew now that, as he was crossing the deserted space in front of the horse corrals and the big ranch house, he was by no means alone.

As he stepped down in front of the hitching rail in front of the log house and wrapped his reins loosely around the blazed log pole, the door opened and a man in a brown Stetson came out.

"I'm here to see Asa Slade," Clint said, his glance quickly taking in the other man's also quick survey of himself.

"I'm Hank Billings, foreman here, remember? Mr. Slade's expecting you."

"Good enough." The Gunsmith nodded and was pleased to see his nod returned. He walked up to the front door as Billings's voice followed him. "Just go right in."

A good man, he decided. And so what was a foreman like Hank Billings doing with riffraff like Holmes and his buddies?

"Asa's just through that door," a slightly raspy voice said out of the semidarkness just inside the entrance.

Clint saw the woman coming toward him.

"I am Dorothy Gilhoon. Asa is expecting you, Mr. Adams."

Clint was surprised to see an attractive woman—not young, yet not wholly middle-aged either—with a warm smile and a firm, decisive carriage. Already, after the meeting with Billings and now this unexpected person, Clint felt his attitude toward Asa Slade becoming more of a question.

There was no question in the mind of Harvey Uriah Whent but that while some men might be universally adjudged as God's gift to women, he unquestionably had to be tagged as God's gift to men.

He was and always had been a man of action. Originally he had come west to organize a territorial university, but, as a bachelor himself, he had swiftly come to the realization that the need for wisdom was less pressing than the need for wives. Forthwith, he had returned east and begun prospecting for eligible female immigrants. With not much difficulty, he induced a dozen adventurous girls to make the arduous journey back to Portland where, as their fresh presence made its expected impression on the local male population, all twelve were shortly happily mated.

Returned to the East, Harvey brimmed with enthusiasm for his Great Plan for East meeting West. He planned bigger and better introductions. Accepting donations to finance a second expedition, he agreed to invest certain sums of money for his backers while back East. In Washington, he even received support from a high political figure who put a steamboat at his disposal.

Brisk with assurance of resounding success for his enterprise, Harvey publicized it widely with notices in the newspapers and with speeches. In a short while, he had some 300 young passengers waiting to venture west into marital bliss. All appeared well. But suddenly, without the slightest warning, one of the big New York newspapers decided to voice its conviction that Mr. Whent was actually a white slaver in clerical clothing and that his flock of innocent, virginal lovelies was headed for the brothels of the wild, wild West. His "cargo" suddenly seemed to vanish into air, with the exception of a suspicious few. Moreover, some of his backers who had been so enthusiastic now demanded the return of their donations. And worse—and all too late—Harvey realized how he had overstepped himself in conferring upon himself the title of "Reverend," plus changing his name to Cornelius Harvey. Exposed, he fled, the situation compounded by the fact that some of the investors' money disappeared with him. He decided that he had not been "dishonest"; he had simply needed the money in order to avoid incarceration, trial, and the Lord knew what all else.

Harvey Whent, like a number of individuals with "light fingers," was prone to weakness, and it was the weakness of habit. His scheme, after all, was such a good one. And to it he returned, but now at a lower notch than that in which he had begun, taking damsels out legitimately as potential brides. Now, as though following some unseen, unwritten law, he began transporting his "merchandise" not to such places as Portland or Seattle but to the brisk cowtowns of the booming West. It followed necessarily that the quality of the goods, while increasing in experience, expertise, and other important areas of human companionship, did lose—by default—certain attributes of the finer elements usually expected of young, "virginal" ladies.

It was better. It was more open—though not publicly open, if he could have put it like that. His cargoes—to Denver, Kansas City, Leadville, Oro Town, Dodge, Cimarron, and other "civilized" towns—were less restrained and more down to earth than they had hitherto been. Although the patina—and this was most important—of respectability and even virginity was upheld and, indeed, emphasized.

Things were going well until Harvey ran into, first, Curfew Bakertone, who included himself into certain aspects of Harvey's action, and now Marshal Noble Studley, who was a great deal less subtle. With the unexpected appearance of Studley, Harvey began to feel just a bit nervous. But he handled the situation, as he admitted to himself, with skill. Harvey had had early training on the riverboats, and he prided himself on his assessment of human character and on his almost flawless timing. And it was timing that now appeared in his move toward mobility in the squeeze he was beginning to experience from Curfew Bakertone and Studley. The expression of this movement appeared in Harvey's sudden realization that his success lay, not in clandestine effort, but in public revelation. It was with this plan in mind that he approached the outspoken, radical warrior of "the western citizenry," Colonel Corliss Witherspoon-Witherspoon.

He found the Colonel in his office on the Main Street of Plains in the midmorning of a fine, cloudless day. The Colonel, trim and neat as a new spool of thread—and that thin, it seemed to Harvey—was sitting at his desk, stroking his white goatee thoughtfully with the thumb and forefinger of his left hand, while with his right he turned a page of the newspaper he was perusing through his narrowed eyes.

"Come in, Mr. Whent. Do come in and join me. I am

about to have a mug of coffee."

It was only then that Harvey realized he had smelled coffee upon entering the tiny office, but he had been taken by the striking figure of the Colonel and so had not noticed.

"That sounds like just the ticket for me," he said warmly, seating himself in the chair toward which his host had waved him with a flip of his long, thin hand.

Meanwhile, the Colonel had risen, grabbed the coffeepot from the top of the stove, and poured into a brace of mugs that were standing on his cluttered desk.

Seated, and after taking a good swig of coffee, he said, "I've just been reading over my story on one of our foremost citizens, and must say I am mightily pleased with it. Even if I do say so myself—who shouldn't." And a round little ball of laughter popped modestly out of his throat, although Harvey Whent, a perspicacious individual all the way to his toe tips, swiftly caught the resonance of self-aggrandizement. Clearly, the Colonel had authored the article in question. Well, reflected the noble partner of Noble Studley—though the relationship would be temporary—he would play the game with Witherspoon Something-or-other as the cards came.

"The story is, of course, concerned with our famous, though highly modest, citizen, Mr. Curfew Bakertone," the Colonel was saying. "No byline; it is, of course, authored by the editor." He was looking at the copy as he spoke and chuckling as he read it silently. "I'll give you a copy, Whent, since I've a similar proposition for yourself."

At this Harvey sat up, almost burning himself with his coffee, which his host had filled to the brim of the mug.

"Uh, how so? I don't quite follow you, Mr. Wither-spoon—or, excuse me—Colonel."

"The name, sir, is Witherspoon-Witherspoon. Colonel Witherspoon-Witherspoon."

"I beg your pardon. I hadn't realized you had a double-barreled monicker, Colonel. When I read it twice like that in your paper the other day, I thought it was a mis-print."

Harvey colored instantly, realizing he'd put not just his foot into it, but his whole leg. "Anyway . . . anyway," he ended up lamely.

The look the Colonel directed to his guest would have withered a fig tree. Harvey Whent said as much silently as he forced himself to look neutral and composed.

"There are a number of persons—and perhaps you know this—a number of persons among the British higher classes who have two names. Hyphenated," the Colonel added, following a short pause. "There are such names as Pryce-Jones, Panter-Alison, Barnstable-Mole. Invariably they are disparate names. In my case, a repetition of the name Witherspoon has occurred."

"Aah, I didn't realize you were English," Harvey said, trying to recover ground.

"I'm from Upper Sandusky, Ohio," the Colonel said.

"Jesus," said Harvey Whent, but to himself.

A brief silence enveloped them as the Colonel folded his paper and took another pull at his coffee.

"It's good coffee," Harvey said pleasantly, feeling the need to keep things going.

"I wish to interview you," the Colonel said. "I am planning a story on your interesting and highly creative enterprise. It would need biographical material, it goes without saying, and other colorful background. This, of course, will be a service to the reading public, not to mention those who are in search of wives. And, uh, I might be able to arrange it so that the charge for this almost national publicity, Mr. Whent, will be minimal." He paused, his pale, oyster-colored eyes regarding Harvey as though he were a specimen of something or other.

Harvey felt his insides sinking as he looked into those pale, creamy orbs. At the same time, the full weight of the atrocious mistake he had made fell on him like a wagonload of rocks. And the terrible thing was that he had walked right into it!

"What a lovely coincidence," Colonel Corliss Witherspoon-Witherspoon was saying. "My coming up with the idea of doing a feature on you, and you walking right in here almost at that very moment. By the way, what was it you wanted to see me about?" He grinned, and Harvey could have sworn it was the grin of a starving wolf upon cornering its quarry. "Don't tell me! Let me guess! I don't have to guess; I'll just bet you came to see me about advertising in the *Plains Endeavor!*"

Harvey sat extremely still in his chair, like a man trying to immobilize himself to stanch the flow of blood just after his throat had been cut.

Bunkered into his chair, the cattle baron looked like one of his own steers. To Clint Adams, Asa Slade was the epitome of the staunch, rugged, dug-in cattleman who wasn't going to give an inch to progress, the wave of immigrants, or the banks, and maybe damn little even to the Almighty. Asa for sure breathed not only air, like everyone else, but fire—unlike everyone else with the exception of a few of his notable compatriots. Men such as Shanghai Pierce, Jesse Chisholm, and John Slaughter.

"I bin expectin' you, Adams." The voice was like a file being rubbed over a broken bottle. "Heard how you come up on the boys and sayin' how you was ramrodding for Miller's MM spread. Now, I want to get a couple things straight."

"So do I," Clint said, stabbing his words right into the middle of the conversation.

"I ain't finished sayin' what I was sayin'," snapped Asa. "I—"

"I haven't even started to begin to finish what I started to say," interrupted Clint.

And the next thing there was a slight rumble in the old rancher's throat and a grin on the Gunsmith's face.

But the moment was brief.

"I have come to check on the MM brand in your gather," Clint said. "That's the size of it."

"You see any?"

"I did. And I didn't have to even get up close."

"I'll believe that when you show me, by God!" snapped Asa. "Where was this?" He cocked his head. "Up by the tableland at Plum Creek?" He was squinting at his visitor, as though weighing something.

"It was by the tableland, and a creek, though I don't know the name of the place."

"Butch there? You know him? Butch?" The eyes were squinting, shrewd and tight on Clint.

"Big fellow."

"Yeah. He's the one, the . . . " But he stopped, and he said, his voice different, "He's ramrodding that north fork there, that stuff. I ain't rid up there in a while; got so much on my hands down here and over by Cottonwood Creek."

"Holmes—Butch—he said he was foreman."

"Sort of like a deppity. Like when Hank Billings ain't around. Hank is foreman of the ZT."

"But Holmes—"

"Holmes gets big for his britches now and again," the rancher cut in. "I'll have to rein him down again."

"He didn't take kindly to my looking over his gather," Clint said.

"Figures."

"Fact, he was downright hostile." Clint kept his eyes squarely on Asa as he spoke, watching for his reaction.

The bushy eyebrows shot up. "We've had a lot of stock rustled this past year, and the boys are tetchy."

"I wouldn't say this without a closer inspection, Slade, but that accusation can work both ways."

The face was suddenly harder. "You sayin' the boys have been running a loose iron, are you?"

"I aim to take a look-see; though by now I reckon ten'll get a man twenty that the evidence ain't."

"Men been shot for sayin' less, Adams!"

"Then why haven't you shot me?"

Asa's milky eyes dropped to the Gunsmith's belt. "First thing, I don't pack hardware."

"But your men do."

"Adams, there is more rustling and horse thieving and God knows what all else goin' on in this part of the country than you can shake a rope at. And it is gettin' worse. A helluva lot worse. Something's got to be done about it. I, for one, am doing what I can. One reason I hired me a extra foreman." He held up a hand to stop Clint from speaking. "Hank Billings is the best ramrod a man could have. He is a top hand and a plus. But he has got two hands and two feet and he can't be everywheres at the same time. How come, like I said, I got me Holmes."

"Who's likely robbing you blind," Clint said, leaning forward with his forearms on his thighs.

The old boy sure didn't like it. Clint could feel his anger like he'd been hit. But there was no point running around the haystack. And all at once he realized that Asa Slade, pioneer cattleman, frontiersman, empire builder, and all the rest of it, was up against something. And sure enough, it came out in the cattleman's next words.

"Thing is, there ain't no law about in Plains or Mile Butte or about anywheres else in this here county of Bullock."

"What about Studley?" Clint pointed out. "I have heard he is a good man. I've heard of him. Got a reputation, even."

"Studley ain't worth what he useta be," Asa said. "Like the rest of us, he got old. Oh, he is still fast; I'd bet on that. He's fast with his gun, but he ain't fast with himself. You know what I am sayin'? He himself ain't fast! And that's what counts. Not just a fast arm and eye and the rest of all that. He is slowed down—and, I'd say, considerable. You foller me?"

"I do. I know exactly what you mean." And he felt a sudden admiration for the old man sitting in front of him. By gosh, that old boy was still fast.

"I hear they call you the Gunsmith," Asa said suddenly.

"I have heard that too," Clint said dryly.

Suddenly a grin had come out of nowhere and was right there in the cattleman's face. "I could say that you be fast, Adams. That is for sure," he added.

"I am what I am," Clint Adams said.

And those simple words fell into the room and stayed there, while the cattleman took a cigar out of his pocket, bit out the little bullet, and then lit up.

"You want one?" He spoke those words around the big Havana that was still in his mouth.

"No."

"Like I said, Studley is older."

Clint was listening to what was behind those words. But he said nothing, and waited for the rancher to go on. He knew what was coming.

"I have heard of you, Adams. What would you say to taking on for the law?"

"I have served my time wearing one of those badges," Clint said. "'Preciate your offer."

"It would have to go by a couple of people. But I could still handle it. We need somebody like yerself."

Clint said nothing.

"What say?"

"I do believe I told you a couple of sentences back what I had to say."

"Shit take it. I had planned to ask you that, you know. It didn't just pop out while we was talking."

"I know."

Suddenly Asa asked, "Want to hear my next offer?"

"The answer is still no. I don't hire my gun."

"A man sharp as yerself could be what would help put this country where it ought to, Adams. You know, we got this goddam rivalry going on about who's gonna be county seat. And it is a real bugger."

Clint was silent for a long moment after Asa finished speaking, waiting for the other man to start up again, but the silence lengthened.

"I reckon I said what I had to," the rancher finally said, knocking the ash of his cigar into a handy cuspidor. "If you be sayin' no like that, then it is no. What else you got to talk about? Tomorrer you can inspect that gather, if you've a mind to."

"'Preciate it," Clint said. And the silence descended again.

Clint waited.

Finally, when the cattleman remained silent, he said, "There is more."

"More?"

"What have you got in your mind, Mr. Slade?"

He saw that he had touched the older man.

"Like I have said, you are a sharp one, Adams."

"I'd say the same for you, Slade. Now tell me, who do you want killed?"

He watched it hit him, right between the eyes. But the old boy stood his ground.

"Who said anything about killing?"

"It's been written all over you," Clint said. "Why else are you talking to me? Why else would your branding crew and that dumb foreman Holmes let me come close enough to see your men were switching brands? You've set this whole thing up. Or somebody has," he added slowly, not taking his eyes off the other man for a second.

Asa Slade sat in his chair, returning the Gunsmith's look; at last he dropped his eyes.

"Who's crowding you?" Clint asked softly.

Asa Slade looked up then, and without a word he reached into his shirt pocket, took out a cigar, and offered it to the Gunsmith.

And this time the Gunsmith took it.

Chapter Seven

"I saw the way you handled that baldheaded man," the lady was saying. "You handled him very well."

Noble Studley let his eyes move away from Constance Bakertone's face as he studied a spot on the wall behind her. He was wondering what in the hell he had gotten himself into. Bakertone! His wife? It had to be.

"I enjoyed it," she was saying.

Studley's eyes moved back to her face, her mouth, her eyes, her mouth again. She had creamy skin; it looked like silk, he was thinking. He looked down at her hand as she lifted her glass. Studley felt it all stirring inside him.

"I suppose you're wondering why I sent for you, Studley."

"It crossed my mind," Studley said dryly.

"I want you to kill somebody," she said calmly, and Studley gulped.

He shifted uneasily in his chair. "I, uh, ain't in that

business, lady. I mean, I am a lawman, a sworn-in officer of the law, which I got to uphold, and so I don't go in for private killing."

"Oh, you wouldn't have to do it yourself. I mean, you could if you wanted to; but it isn't necessary. What I'm offering you is the job of planning, finding the person to execute the job—carry it out—and see that nobody is any the wiser. But of course, first we have to find the person who needs to be killed. That is to say, punished."

Studley realized suddenly that his mouth was hanging open. The cool effrontery of what the woman was saying chilled him. It was as though his veins were suddenly filled with water. At the same time, there was a kind of fire in him. He could neither explain it nor describe it, and he didn't try. He only knew that he was gripped by something right beyond his control and his understanding.

He shifted in his chair. "I think you've come to the wrong person." And he started to get to his feet.

"Sit down, Marshal." Her smile transformed her suddenly. She gave a laugh—musical, light as air, as though the two of them were sharing a beautiful day. "I was only testing you, sir. I'm sorry. I didn't want you to kill anybody. I don't even think of that kind of activity myself."

Studley heard himself saying, "But you said also something about planning, about getting someone to do something. You see, as an officer of the law, I will have to report this talk we're having." He wondered, fleetingly, whether she was crazy.

"I know that, Studley." She said the name as though trying it on for size. "You know, I've always liked the

name Studley. *Noble Studley.* It's an interesting name."
She gave an amused laugh, then pursed her lips.

They were very red, Studley noted.

"Studley," she said the name again. "Noble Studley."
And suddenly there was something else in her smile.
"Tell me, whatever happened to Prior Studley?"

He had been waiting for it. He had felt it coming as
soon as she'd started playing with his name. And he
was not surprised, for he had long since accepted the
fact that someone, somewhere, some day, would come
up with just that question.

She was smiling at him, but it was a smile that had
been painted on her face. A smile that was part of her
act. But somehow, he knew she didn't know the whole
story. She wouldn't have brought it up in that way if she
had known the whole of it. Not like that. And yet, was
that certain? Studley wanted to get up and walk away,
but somehow he continued to sit there. Then, suddenly
remembering his drink, he lifted his glass and very nearly
drained it.

She was looking at him with an amused expression
on her face.

Studley said, "I don't know what you're talking about.
Maybe there is somebody else about with the same name
as mine, but I don't know about it." He stood up, lifted
his glass, and finished off his drink.

"Think it over," she said, as he walked to the door.
"Mr. Bakertone is very interested in the fact that you
have the same name as someone both he and myself
knew some years ago."

"And where is this person now?" Studley asked.

"That is what we both would like to know."

Studley continued to stand there, looking at her seated in her chair.

"That is what we, and also the law, would like to know." And then, suddenly, a laugh broke from those red lips. "You see, Studley, the other Studley disappeared."

"I know nothing about that," Studley said.

"Mr. Bakertone—and I, too—are very concerned about getting it all straightened out. Especially now, with the election coming up."

"The election?"

"For the county seat. Remember?"

"Sure."

"My husband thought you might be interested in running for mayor of Plains."

"Plains? Why Plains?"

"Everything seems to point to Plains winning out for the county seat. Wouldn't you agree?"

"I dunno."

"Being mayor could be a good job."

"For the mayor?" he said suddenly, his lips tight.

She gave a laugh. "For whoever is in the right place at the right time."

Studley decided he'd gone far enough. "Listen," he said. "If your husband wants me to run for mayor, he can ask me himself. You got it?" He had found his anger at last, and it felt good. Even though he knew he was a bit shaky.

"Mr. Bakertone is a very busy man, Studley. And I suggest you think it all over and don't act hastily. Don't forget that my husband and I are both very interested in what happened to Prior Studley."

"He was my brother," Studley said, barely moving his lips. "He's dead."

"How did he die?"

"That ain't your business," Studley said, standing up and pushing back his chair with his leg. "Prior is dead."

"I think it *is* my business, sir." And suddenly her tone of voice was as hard as his, while her eyes glared.

Studley had started to turn toward the door to leave the room, but her face, her tone, stopped him.

"You really are Bakertone's missus?"

"I am."

Studley realized he'd been holding his lighted cigar that she had given him; he realized it when she lifted her own cigar and drew on it.

Studley felt that moment in a way he'd not felt a good many other things in his life.

"I work rather closely with my husband," she said now, looking then at the ash as she tapped it off her cigar. Then she raised her eyes to Studley. "Of course, Curfew has other business of his own, as I also have other business of my own. Right now, I've been asked to, shall we say, sound you out. In a sort of way. Test your mettle. There is important work ahead."

"I've already been working with Bakertone," Studley said, moving a step closer to the table.

"I know." She smiled suddenly, though Studley felt no warmth from it. "Studley, sit down."

He took a step toward his vacated chair and put his hand on its back, but he remained standing.

"Stubborn," she said. And her laugh was rich, but without real humor. "You see, there is big work, and we have to be sure of the men we're working with. I am sure you can understand it." She laid her cigar on the edge of the table and then, leaning on her forearms, laced her fingers together in front of her.

"And so it's been necessary to test certain elements. For instance, you have—or had—the reputation of being what is called a top gun. It was necessary to check on this. Curfew, as you know, arranged it so you were appointed a deputy marshal, then full marshal. But he—we both—felt it was necessary to be sure you were really what you were supposed to be."

"Geeker," Studley said.

She nodded. "As I said, you handled that well. Geeker was really gunning for you."

Studley's tone of voice was grating as he said, "Did I pass the test, then?"

"I believe so." She let her eyes rest on the bridge of his nose. "You see, at the beginning, when Curfew contacted you, he was sure of you, but I wasn't."

Her eyes were level with his as she said those words.

"Why not?" Studley asked.

She kept her eyes on his, without moving, as she spoke. "You might say my husband and I sometimes see things and people a little differently."

"I see," Studley said, though he didn't.

"You see, Curfew reasoned that any man who would kill his own brother was capable of, well, anything." She paused, watching Studley's face turn white, then darken.

Studley said, "And you?"

"Me? Me, I was not so sure. Not so sure that you would stand up in a, shall we say, more even-Steven situation; if I could put it like that." Her words were like chips of ice.

"So you got Geek—" Studley's voice didn't last through the whole sentence, and he had to clear his throat and repeat, "Geeker."

"Yes. Geeker—was all right." She picked up her cigar and took a drag on it. "You could be the kind of mayor that the people would want. Or you could not." She paused. "Somebody will contact you to let you know what to do."

Studley didn't say anything.

"Well . . . ?" She was looking at him through the little cloud of smoke from her cigar.

More than anything, Studley wanted to say no, or say that he would think about it, or tell her to go to hell and take her goddamn husband with her. More than anything . . .

He thought of Geeker; Geeker from the old days. And then, to his astonishment, he found himself thinking of the Gunsmith. It was a thought that moved him to the door, and he was able at least to leave without saying anything.

He had thrown his duffel near the big cottonwood that was closest to the creek. It was still daylight, and for a moment or two he seriously considered riding back to see Tony Miller, but he knew there was a chance that Butch and his buddies might follow him there. The less they were in the area of the MM the better, was how he looked at that. On the other hand, he wanted very much to see the girl.

At any rate, he reminded himself, Tony and her young

brother, Andy, had been all right thus far—as far as any visit from Butch Holmes and the boys went. And so he put that little thread of concern out of his mind.

Now, seated on his bedroll crosslegged, he watched the long light slipping over the land, through the bunch grass, through the box elders and willows running along the creek bank, lighting on Duke's rump and withers where he'd staked him.

All at once his thoughts were on his friend Hank Sayles, whom he'd not seen in some while. He wondered how Hank was doing. The last talk they'd had cleared a lot of things for Clint regarding the situation in Plains and in Mile Butte.

They had been sitting at a table in the Ace Saloon, a drinking establishment that, Clint had discovered, served passable whiskey. He would have liked a good stiff whiskey right now, he was thinking, as he sat on his bedroll and began to feel the chill of the evening deepening. But he was no drinker, really, and that thought passed as he began to focus on his recapitulation of the scene with Hank Sayles.

Hank had been telling him why he'd written; he'd really had no suspicion of trouble at that moment, but rather, something indefinable had been nagging at him. Clint had nodded, understanding now the ambiguity of Hank's note. Clearly, Hank had a hunch—almost, but not quite, a notion—but not yet a formed thought that something was strange in the situation in which he was finding himself.

"Bakertone hired me, or leastways invited me to come have a look-see. And then he just handed me the land surveyor's office. Feller named Bill Ketchum had been doing it. Disappeared; some think he fell into the Naco Ravine up around Twenty Creek. Some used to think something else, but that died out."

"That there was something else going on," Clint put in.

Hank nodded. "Something. Anyhow, there I was, and here I am. Bakertone—and, by the way, he has got a wild missus—the two of them laid it out to me."

"What is it?" Clint asked. "Did Bakertone say how he and his company want to move in and exploit Plains, Mile Butte, and probably the whole of Bullock County, and maybe even more?"

"Not like that; not in so many words. But I got the drift that there was something big behind his operation. I mean, bigger than what he let on."

"Could you explain that a little more?" Clint asked. "Seems to me that something gave you that cold feeling, but you weren't sure just what."

Hank nodded, his face thoughtful as he tried to form what was coming into his mind. "It wasn't all that clear. See, everything seemed on the up and up. They—the company, New England Cattle, Land & Transportation— wanted to build some more; make more what Bakertone called 'improvements.' And they were getting, so he said, clearance from Washington."

"And he told you how that would build the country, and civilize the Wild West, and give people jobs, and make a lot of money all round," Clint put in.

Hank grinned ruefully at that. "You have heard the story before, just as I have. It all sounded on the straight. Only at some point—I'm not sure where—I began to catch a faint smell of something like a rat. And even now it's hard to put my finger on it."

"I know just what you mean. You know something's wrong, but you don't know how to say it." Clint paused then. He remembered it now as he brought it back to himself, the scene with Hank, the appearance of the saloon, even the smell of the place, trying to see if there was something he had missed—or for that matter, that Hank had overlooked.

If anything, it seemed to him now, as he looked back, that Hank Sayles had been a bit nervous or even worried. It didn't seem like him; but there it was. And the impression had lingered with the Gunsmith.

And then Hank had said he'd been wondering if maybe he was feeling spooky about the whole deal because he hadn't found anything of especial interest during his surveying, and yet he'd had the definite feeling that Bakertone expected him to find something.

"But you found nothing?" Clint said.

"Not a thing. Just what you usually find when you survey: a good bit of measurement and information on the quality of the land in question."

"Like gold, maybe?" Clint asked suddenly.

"Gold! Why do you say gold?"

"Because it's what everybody seems to be hoping he will find out in this country."

"Not around here," Hank said firmly.

"Hasn't it been discovered in even unlikelier places?" Clint argued.

Hank had to nod at that. "True enough," he said. And then that reminded him of something. "You know, there have been rumors about the possibility of gold up around Gopher. Gopher's on the other side of Beaker Valley, not too far from the Gold Hills, where there was a strike, as you likely know."

"But the Gold Hills have been mined out," Clint said. "Am I right on that?"

"You are. But you know there've been rumors and all that talk ever since. People want a gold strike! Let's face it. Clint, I've been around the country as long as you have. Both of us have been all over—north, south, east, west. You name it, and we've seen it. Not to sing a brag on it, but it's a fact. And I am telling you I don't bite easy on a thing. But there is definitely something going on, and I can't figure what."

"And for sure, there isn't just gold strikes going on," Clint said. "There have been plenty of false gold rushes."

"There's a damn fool born every minute," Hank agreed. "Hell, remember the Big Lucky?"

"The two old boys who took the Bank of San Francisco and those big men in Wall Street and London?"

"The Frame brothers."

They both had a laugh at that. How the brothers Frame, two old sourdough types, had ambled into the swanky Stock Hotel in San Francisco and deposited a sack in the hotel safe. The sack containing a mess of gold nuggets. The old boys asking the clerk not to let anybody near it but to make sure it was in the safest possible place.

Both Clint and Hank chuckled as they recounted the outrageous adventure of the Frame brothers.

"You can bet your ass that room clerk kept his mouth shut for about as long as it took him to get to somebody important," said Hank. "Probably took an hour or two before the whole bag of suckers had the news."

"They took the head of the Bank of San Francisco, I heard," Clit said.

"And the boys in New York, Boston, and even in London."

"Two dumb prospecting yokels," Clint said, as they both had a good chuckle.

"Those yokels—by God, the law couldn't lay a finger on them when the whole thing blew. You know that?"

"That's what I heard," Clint said. "On account of they had never said they had any gold or had a strike or anything."

"Salted by God, right down to the last grain!" And Hank Sayles nearly fell out of his chair, laughing at the way the two "hicks" had taken the big boys, just like they were the veriest rubes.

"They salted every inch of it," Hank went on. "Then just played it dumb and innocent, letting those smart-aleck Frisco and New York bankers beg them to sell the whereabouts of their strike."

"I heard they held out, fought against selling it," Clint said. "For sure with each refusal the price went up. I heard it was one big helluva lot of money."

"They got away with it, clean as a whistle." Hank Sayles's big jaw dropped wide open with awe as he said those words.

Then Clint said, "You have got any notion such a caper might be going on around here?"

"I dunno. But I wouldn't bet against it. Not with a sharp sonofabitch like that beanpole Bakertone and that great-looking bitch he's got for a wife. Nothing would surprise me from that pair."

"What's he really after?" Clint asked.

"Dunno. He moved out here only a little while back. Came out from Chicago. Moved in and became the number-one citizen. Like he was the only man ever heard of the Declaration of Independence. A real thumper when it came to making speeches on the wonders of the West and all that. Meanwhile, he worked his way into running the bank, the school, a number of saloons, not to mention the town council."

"Somebody said he even runs the church," Clint said with a wry grin.

"I wouldn't bet against it. He's always making speeches, but at the same time he doesn't spread himself in public."

"You're saying he works behind, in the background."

Hank was nodding. "I do. He is someone more felt than actually seen. Then, of course, he's helped some families. He is generous. I know about an old couple he staked. I've heard of other situations where he's been downright generous. But I wonder just how much that's true generosity and how much is paving his way for something else. And I know that sounds shitty to doubt a man who comes across when a family's in need. But Bakertone don't look to me like a feller who'd do a single damn thing less he was getting something out of it."

Clint then asked him again if he thought there could be a big swindle afoot, pointing out that there were trainloads of immigrants coming into the country and that the railroads and land companies had been advertising for them.

"I dunno, my friend," Hank said. "I don't know. But I feel something, and that's why I wrote you. You know, let me just say one thing. When I work out a survey, I am putting my reputation on the line. That's what Johnnie Knowles did when he caught those two Frame brothers—or, I should say, caught their action. Like I said, the law couldn't do a thing to them. They had sold nothing. The greeners and marks had insisted on buying in. But Johnnie was the one who found the place and exposed the whole thing. And he said that to me when he was telling me about it one time down in Fort Worth. He was a good man, let me tell you, and he told me how he could have sold out, left the thing alone, even worked something to his own advantage. But he remembered surveying isn't a cheap thing. Like I say, you put yourself on the line."

Now, as he pondered that scene with his old friend, Clint found himself wondering. There was still something missing. First of all, he told himself, he hadn't yet really seen why Hank Sayles had written him. For there didn't seem to be a problem that Hank couldn't handle himself. But when he tried pressing the question in that direction, he got nowhere. All Hank would say was that he had a hunch that something wasn't "right." But he could give no evidence.

And yet, it was in his tone somehow, his attitude; it was not in his actual words. There was something too vague, something that Hank was obviously feeling very strongly but was not able to express.

And then, all at once, the Gunsmith realized what it was: Hank Sayles was afraid. And it was a bad one. Hank was scared as hell. The Gunsmith would have bet his last cartridge on it.

* * *

"I still feel that the best thing is to hire somebody." It was Constance Bakertone speaking, her oval face shining with earnestness as she tried again to get her point through.

Curfew was shaking his head even before she'd finished speaking. This habit of his always infuriated her. But this time she managed to control herself, only because of the importance of the point she wished to get across.

"But why not?" she insisted. "I cannot see why you object to my suggestion. We have both agreed that Adams is going to be trouble. And it's right before your eyes, Curfew. He's a friend of Sayles. And—you heard it—they've been talking together. You heard what that man said."

"What man?" He looked casually at her, looking along his nose, with his head back, as he sat at his desk. And for a moment his eyes dropped to her bosom, which was always a pleasure, but then he returned to her face. She was frowning.

"I'm referring to the big man; something with an H. His name, I mean."

"Holmes. Yes. Of course." He cleared his throat, looking for something handy, but the spitoon was not where he expected it to be, so he returned his attention to his wife. "Butch Holmes," he said.

"Couldn't he handle it?"

Curfew was again shaking his head. "No one man can go up against somebody of Adams's caliber, my dear. And anyway, it's essential to plan something, to bring some sort of surprise. I trust, uh, that you will trust me to be sufficiently intelligent and able to run my business. Eh? Huh?" And his mouth opened as though in a laugh, but there was no humor apparent.

Constance Bakertone sighed with frustration. But she knew better than to stand by her guns. No matter which way you went with Curfew, you were going to end up losing. She wondered how she'd stood it this long.

"Something is being arranged to remove Mr. Adams from the scene. Our friend Studley is working on it."

"I don't trust Studley," Constance said.

Her husband suddenly flashed a rare grin at her. "My dear, it is quite unnecessary to trust anyone. In fact, it's the wise man who doesn't. As I have often told you, Constance, trust only yourself; then you'll know who stabbed you in the back."

She sighed, having heard this tiring bit of wisdom a few dozen or so times already.

Bakertone watched her. "Everything is being arranged. And, even more," he added, in a quieter voice and as an afterthought.

"You're saying that you have further plans, is that it?" Her tone was sharper than she had intended, but she didn't retreat. She hated the way he would always engage her in his plans, but would then keep special parts to himself. In a word, he took from her only what he needed and didn't really share a thing. It infuriated her, but she was helpless. The fact that she was helpless only made her more angry, especially as she realized that she was afraid of him.

And it amused Curfew Bakertone no end to see how she tried to hide her fear of him. Of course, many people feared him, but he found that his wife's discomfort was especially nourishing.

"I have work to do, my dear," he said abruptly, pulling

himself in toward his desk and reaching for a piece of paper.

Constance rose swiftly to her feet, her mouth set in firm denial of his rudeness. "I had thought you wanted to go over the plan," she said.

"I did," he said, without looking up from the piece of paper he was scanning. "I did. And we did," he added with a little sigh, as he reached for a pen to make a note on the paper he was reading.

He thought she had turned to leave, but suddenly she was standing just behind him and had put her hand on his shoulder. He didn't move; he went on reading.

"Curfew . . . "

"Hmm . . . " He did not take his eyes from the paper.

"Curfew, my dear. It's been rather a while since . . . "

He put down his pen, turned, and looked at her. "Yes, I am terribly busy, though. As you can see."

"But—"

"Later . . . my dear. I must get this work done, or we'll all end up—well, where will we end up?" He gave a little popping sound with his mouth, trying to turn it all into a laugh.

"Tonight?"

"If you're not too tired, my dear."

Her mouth fell open. "If I am not too tired!"

They both gave a laugh at that. A dutiful, marital laugh, the kind of laugh that had so often recemented their marriage in a difficult moment.

He watched her leave, smiling at her as she nodded a good-bye, and then closed the door behind her.

He returned to his paper, and ten minutes later there came a knock at his door.

"Come," he called out, and, placing his pen carefully on his desk, he looked up to face Noble Studley.

"I'm pretty busy, Studley." And then he worked his jaws, moving his mouth around as though searching for a piece of elusive food. "Unless, of course, it's about the business we discussed."

"It's about Candy O'Toole," Studley said, his face as expressionless as a door.

"What about Miss O'Toole?" Curfew said.

"Herself and her girls have got theirselves in a uproar over Harvey and *his* girls."

Curfew leaned back in his chair now, his eyebrows lifted, as he reached to his waistcoat pocket and brought out a wooden toothpick. "What about?"

"About them girls of Harvey's cuttin' in on their business," Studley said, making no effort to disguise the surprise in his voice at Bakertone's slow understanding.

"Studley, I understand perfectly," Curfew said softly. His voice was purring as he added, "Even though I am now and again dimwitted."

Studley got the point.

"What you want to do about it?" Studley asked. "They claim as how not a one of 'em is gonna put out if that kind of thing keeps up. I am only telling you what Candy told me. I am only passing it on."

"But what the hell do they want me to do?" Curfew asked. "I can't help them. Except I know if they pull something like that it'll shove a war at us." He leaned back in his chair, his eyes discovering a random design on the ceiling.

"Studley, you handle it. I have more important matters

to attend to." He dropped his eyes to the man standing in front of his desk. "The other matter that we spoke about. You're on it?"

"Yup. Exceptin' it ain't gonna be easy."

"I never suggested that it would be. But I want you to have everything ready, just in the event that we need to move in that direction. You understand? Don't do anything; don't make any move toward our, uh, target. But be ready to act on an instant's notice. You got that?"

"I do. But I want to say again, it's got to be like I ain't in it. Like you agreed to."

"If I agreed to it, then, Studley, there is no need for you to raise the question." The words fell from those dry lips like pieces of ice.

Studley said, "There is the election for county seat coming up."

"Thanks for telling me." This time the words were like frozen blades. "I do believe that I am aware of that fact."

"What I am saying is if you want, I'll agree to run for mayor when it's decided to vote on that part of it."

Bakertone turned his face toward Studley then. "I knew you would, Noble. I knew you wouldn't let us down."

The use of his first name shocked Studley into almost stammering. "I am only doing that, only agreeing to that, because—"

But Curfew Bakertone cut him off, sharply. "Because—to invent a new way of saying it—because I know where the body is buried, Studley. I don't know why, but that isn't necessary to know—The fact of your brother's, uh, mysterious death. And, yes, on second thought, I believe I do know why. It's obvious—to *me*. And I can even sympathize with you. But that's all unnecessary to go into now. What is necessary in this short—or long— life, Studley, is to know the people you deal with. Each man—and there are no exceptions, Studley—each man has a weak place. Do you agree with that? You of all people certainly should agree. Now then, Studley. This is the question for us to find out—or, rather, for you to find out. Do you know what it is?" His eyebrows rose in an arch, his hairy nostrils dilated; he lifted his chin, almost as if inviting Studley to take a swat at it. "Eh?"

"The Gunsmith? Clint Adams?"

"We are not talking about George Washington."

"Huh?" Studley said. And then again: "Huh?"

"That's enough for now," Curfew said, and his attention dropped again to his desk as he sat forward.

Studley had reached the door. He turned, his hand dropping away from the doorknob.

"I have got a notion," he said.

"Tell me about it when it is ready to bear fruit."

"It's ready any time," Studley said. "Any time you're— we're—ready to go ahead with the rest of the plan." He turned back to the door and put his hand on the knob.

Somewhere a grandfather clock was striking the hour. It came clearly into the office, but neither man paid it any attention. They continued to stand there, looking at each other.

The clock finished its toll.

"Well?" Curfew was drumming the fingers of his right hand on his desktop.

"You want to know what it is, I'll tell you," Studley said, enjoying himself as he took his time. It was real good to get some of his own back.

He licked his lips with the tip of his tongue. "Adams has a big weakness. His horse. I remember hearing it from the old days when I was around Santa Fe. And Butch reminded me of it when he told how when he run into Adams out at Miller's MM. Adams got real feisty when Butch admired his big black gelding."

And once again Studley beamed inside himself for scoring as he saw the silent laughter coming into Curfew Bakertone's eyes.

Chapter Eight

"Thank you."

Clint had started to fall asleep, and the words whispered in his ear brought him back to the girl beside him. To Tony.

"Thank you," he said, turning his face toward her but keeping his eyes closed.

Her hand had started moving along his arm, and now he reached over and touched the inside of her thigh. It was still damp from their lovemaking.

"I'm so happy you came by," she said.

"Heck, I'm supposed to be the foreman of this outfit, aren't I?" he said, sliding his erection between her legs. "What's called the ramrod of the outfit."

Her laughter tinkled against the side of his face as he came over on top of her and her legs moved apart.

He entered her smoothly. She was very wet, already slippery with the juice of their recent passion.

Now his strokes were long and slow, drawing out

almost to the tip of his tool, and then sliding all the way up to the point where their hair rubbed joyously together. She began to moan.

Then she said, "We'd best be careful, quiet, or Andy will think something's going on."

"It is," he said.

"We don't want him to come in."

"You locked the door. Don't worry."

"Oh, I'm not worrying. I'm not worrying. I'm not worrying. . . . "

And their bodies began to undulate more quickly as one body; a single overwhelming passion had taken hold of them, and they were ecstatically helpless.

Now their tempo increased and they were stroking quickly, as his organ grew even thicker, longer at the bursting point. She never missed her stroke either and stayed right with him, faster and faster and deeper, as their bodies opened even more with the coursing of their ecstasy which now controlled them completely.

Until at last they came, squirting their love juices as one bursting fountain of bliss. Then they slowly subsided, savoring the last exquisite drops until they all but blanked out—and maybe they did, for all they knew—until now, knowing not a thing except that superb dying-in-life, that ultimate reach of love and passion.

They lay wrapped in the silence of her bed, her room, the house, and the great starry night surrounding them.

And all at once the Gunsmith was wide awake. He listened. And he heard it again. In a trice, he was out of bed and stepping into his clothes.

"What is it?" Tony asked, sitting up.

The moonlight was at the windowsill, and he could

see her outline; naked, beautiful. But he had no time for desire as he pulled on his boots.

"Stay here. No, better get into Andy's room."

"You heard something? Maybe it's Andy."

"I don't think so. But I'll see. Do as I say."

And he was gone. Standing still in the dark house outside her bedroom door. Listening.

He heard it again. It was outside the house. Swiftly he crossed the living room and entered the kitchen. Fortunately, the moonlight was not on that side of the building, and it was reasonably dark. However, he could see clearly through the window. He could see the horse corral, the barn. Quickly, but without hurry, he checked through all the windows. He saw nothing unusual. Yet the feeling was that strong that he returned to the kitchen and waited by the window, watching the barn. He was thinking of Butch Holmes and his two sidekicks, and the time that Holmes had been looking at Duke, commenting on what a fine piece of horseflesh he was.

Clint quickly checked his Winchester, then stepped through the kitchen and slipped through a door on the other side of the house, where the moonlight was weakest.

He stood outside the cabin now, listening. Nothing. He studied the sky. It was getting toward dawn.

He waited, listening, and now heard nothing. Still he remained. Presently he heard the horse galloping away toward the creek. There was no sense in giving chase. By the time he got Duke saddled and bridled, the intruder would be well gone.

Duke! And he remembered again the big, beefy Butch Holmes with his sneer, his tiny eyes, and the way he had looked at the big black horse.

Duke was staked where he'd left him, away from the house—not far, but hidden from the house, and, indeed, from any approach by the surrounding cottonwoods and box elders.

It wasn't light enough to find tracks, but as far as he could tell, the visitor hadn't been near the horse. Nor did Duke seem in any way spooked. Clint stood close to him, while the big black nuzzled him. Then he decided to take a look in the barn.

The sky was beginning to lighten in the east as he walked into the log barn. Then he saw the paper on the side of the stall. It had been pulled down on a spike that was there for rigging. But it hadn't been pulled over the spike with any care; in fact, it seemed whoever had done it had hurried, for the paper was almost cut in two.

The letter was hand-printed: "Leave the country, Gunsmith, or your friends will pay."

The eastern sky was readying for the sun as he walked to the house and entered the kitchen. Tony was waiting for him.

"Andy's still asleep," she said. She was wearing an old woolen bathrobe, with a belt that had tassles on each end. It was tied together at her waist.

Clint showed her the message that had been in the barn.

"Well, that's pretty plain," she said.

"It sure is."

"Do you have any idea who might have left it?"

"Somebody who's afraid of me. But his name? I'd have to make it up." He smiled gently at her, realizing suddenly how lovely she was, especially in that aged bathrobe.

"I'm a mess," she said, suddenly realizing how he was looking at her.

"You're damn good-looking, and you know it," he said firmly, with a grin. "Now then, how about some coffee? Then it'll be light enough for me to do some studying on the situation."

She had turned toward the stove. "How will you do that?" she asked over her shoulder, as she lifted some kindling from the stack nearby.

"I'll look for sign. But I'll also be thinking. Somebody is mighty anxious for me to get shut of this country. I wonder if it has anything to do with you."

She was bent over the stove, having just removed a lid so that she could build the fire for their coffee. "How me? Why do you think it's something to do with me? Because you're the MM foreman? But that was only for a day."

"As far as I am concerned, ma'am, it is for the duration of this here trouble over land, cattle, maybe even water, for all we know."

"Water!" She turned to face him, a wooden lucifer in her hand, ready to light some pitch that she had fed into the big kitchen range. "What made you think of water?"

"On account of I was thinking of gold," he said simply.

She stared at him, her mouth slightly open in astonishment. "Mr. Adams, are you tetched? Gold! Water!"

He smiled at her; then he was swiftly serious. "When there ain't enough water about, young lady, then water is worth more than gold. See, gold might appear to a lot of people to be like life and death. But water is actually life and death. Make no mistake about that."

"But there's plenty of water here," she insisted, still staring at him in great surprise.

"Maybe." He nodded toward the stove. "How's that coffee coming?"

There were tracks, especially near the barn, where the horse had stepped in manure. The rider apparently had made little effort to conceal his trail. Yet there were no tracks around the area where he had staked Duke.

Standing just outside the barn, Clint studied the situation and found his thoughts on the rider who had apparently been following him when he'd ridden after Butch Holmes and his buddies. He remembered clearly the track the man's horse had left. Strange, remembering that. This was enough to bring him back to the pile of manure outside the barn. He couldn't have sworn to it, yet it was damn close. Still, it was also memory, and memory was not always satisfactory. Yet there was also something else, a sort of feeling he had about the whole thing. The mystery rider—whoever it was—was clearly interested in himself. And he was sure he was not part of the Butch Holmes bunch. Who, then?

He said nothing of this to Tony when he returned to the kitchen for coffee. For he was near-dead certain that the rider was concerned with himself. Yet, it couldn't be a drygulcher. If he was in that category, then why hadn't he taken a shot at his target? No, whoever it was had come to watch him, in both instances. Possibly the first time he had been scared off by the proximity of Holmes and his boys, and now at the MM—by what? The coming daylight?

"What are you thinking about so?" the girl suddenly

asked as she sat down again at the table to join him.

"Just the situation."

"Why Asa Slade wants the MM?"

"That's no question. He wants it for protection or to sell to someone and make a profit. It's always the same story: land-grabbing for the benefit of the grabber. Right?"

She gave a rueful smile and nodded.

"Anyway," he went on, half thinking it aloud for himself, "somebody interested in getting the MM—a man such as Slade—wouldn't need to come and take a look at the outfit, would he?"

She gave a little laugh at that. "I certainly wouldn't think so. He knows the MM almost as well as the ZT. It used to be part of his outfit years ago."

"Did it?" He sat up a bit at that. "Long ago? When would you say?"

"Before I was born, or perhaps right after. A good while," she said, coloring a little.

"It can't be all that while back," Clint said, smiling at her.

"Flattery, Mr. Adams, is one of your strong points, I see." And they both had a laugh at that.

"Except—and get this straight, miss—I was not flattering you. Now, we will not mention the subject again; until, well, maybe later." He stood up. "I just want to check something out by the barn."

"Yessir," she said, snapping her words out like a soldier.

He made a funny face at her as he went to the door.

Outside, he left the funning for a moment and became again the man of the trail, the tracker, hunter, warrior, with every nerve and muscle in his body in contact with the whole of his attention.

Yes, there was something he had seen by that footprint, something that had caught the corner of his vision and stuck there, plucking at him.

Squatting, he picked it up. It was a button. And it was off an army coat. He studied it, recognizing that it was a Confederate button and probably from a greatcoat, judging from the size of it.

Of course, it could be coincidence and not have been left by the horsebacker at all. All the same, he had the definite feeling that this was not so. He was certain that the button had come from the man whose horse had left the hoofprint.

Within moments he had saddled and bridled Duke, but then on a sudden impulse, he stripped the horse. Now, painstakingly, he covered every inch of Duke's big body, looking for any sign that would indicate injury. And he found nothing. Then he saddled and bridled him and led him up to the house. Tony came out just as he reached the door.

"You and Andy keep your eyes open," he said, his voice grave with warning.

"Clint, what's wrong? Please tell me!"

"Nothing that I can put my hand on," he said gently, putting his hands on her shoulders and looking down into her deep eyes. "As far as I can see, everything's all right at the MM. But I want you to take care."

"Why all this mystery, then?"

"I've got a hunch. Something. I can't say anything's actually wrong, because then by naming it I'd know what it was. And I don't know."

She was nodding, picking up on it instantly. "Yes, I know that kind of thing. I often wonder about that—that kind of knowing something without actually knowing it in words."

"So I'm just playing my hunch," Clint said. "I don't want to close down on something and then make a stupid mistake. I like to leave it open, so that I can see what's actually happening."

"I understand you."

She was looking up into his eyes.

"Yes, I can see you do," he said.

He bent down and their lips met.

"I love to kiss you," she said. "It's sweet."

"I'll have to remember to kiss you again, then," he said. And this time his kiss was longer and deeper.

And so was hers.

Suddenly there was a parade! Everyone was instantly thrown into an excitement that they hadn't known for some time, not since Stella Harvey gave birth to twins. But Stella Harvey's was not a production to compare with the county-seat parade.

"Of course, the ballot boxes were stuffed, and you know that a goodly number of votes were cast by people who never existed; but the other side was doing the same!"

It was, of course, Colonel Corliss Witherspoon-Witherspoon offering his latest dissertation on some aspect of the world; this time in the office of his *Plains Endeavor*, while Clint Adams listened in silent respect to the Great Man who—to quote his very own words—"had brought a free newspaper to the frontier, an organ of candid opinion and fact, representing the fighting voice of Democracy and fairmindedness in this new and thrilling nation!"

"Etcetera. . . . " Clint Adams muttered to himself, as he listened to the Colonel declaiming in his stentorian voice.

Clint had decided to visit the editor and publisher of the "Voice of Freedom," hoping to come upon some clue or lead in the flow of philosophy, politics, science, literature, and common and uncommon sense that rushed forth to encompass wholly—and often even drown—whatever subject might happen to arise.

In the present case, of course, it had to relate to the action in which the Gunsmith found himself. Clint was taking a gamble, because he knew very well that while a man such as the Colonel had his hand and his tongue on a great many stories, gossip, scandals, and even dangerous disclosures, he was a man who undoubtedly knew how to feather his own nest, and no matter at whose expense.

They had both seen the great parade, standing near each other, Clint having deliberately arranged that he would, as it were, bump into the Colonel.

The news of the parade, of course, had spread like a prairie fire throughout the two towns of Plains and Mile Butte, the action taking place on the eve of the election.

The Gunsmith had been witness to a number of parades in his time, but the one for the "election" of the county seat of Bullock County was one of the most extraordinary, as well as most enjoyable. And whoever had organized it—everyone, of course, realizing it was done under the auspices of Curfew Bakertone—had the genius to produce the event by torchlight.

Clint had ridden into town that afternoon, and, having made the decision to casually run into Witherspoon-Witherspoon, he was just looking for the right moment. He could already sense an excitement in the Plains air as the sun was going down.

Not long after nightfall, Main Street began to fill with people. The streetlights were lit, and the lights in the various saloons and gaming halls added to the excitement of the coming evening. Overhead, the sky was dotted with stars. And in hardly any time at all, the sidewalks and a good bit of the street itself were packed and even overflowing.

The crowd was noisy. Their loud conversation and occasional shouts and laughter rivaled the clamor coming from the dancehalls and saloons.

Someone had worked out a plan with great care. Early on—and Clint discovered this later in conversation with the Colonel—certain men began to filter into the crowd, leaving their gaming tables and usual nightly activities to mingle with the crowd. These men were spread about, but working in couples. Their purpose was to talk up Plains as the better choice for county seat. But they had been ordered to speak carefully and not provoke violence. This was a necessary though important caution, for, in fact, there were actual fisticuff encounters over the "burning issue." Yet, they were clever. One of the pair would open a loud conversation with his confederate, a question about the coming election, using the other's reply as an opening wedge to sell Plains as county seat.

They spoke loudly, thus attracting the attention of all around them. It was, Clint realized, the fine art of shilling, so dear to every carnival and bunco artist throughout the West.

Suddenly there came a great shout down at one end of Main Street, triggering a mighty roar from the crowd lining the sidewalks; followed by the banging of a big bass drum.

Somebody shouted, "Here they come!" And Clint, moving closer to Colonel Witherspoon-Witherspoon, felt the crowd stiffen and begin to churn with excitement.

The bass drum was pounding more loudly now, accompanied by some fiddles and banjos and a fife. Glassjaw McRooney, a bareknuckler of the old school of prizefighting, was leading the band, sawing magnificently on his fiddle as he danced down the street. A roar greeted him as the crowd realized he was sawing his fiddle with a nail.

A lean giant of a man marched close behind him, blowing his cornet, his cheeks puffed out hard as billiard balls, his lean body and huge flat feet keeping marvelous tempo with his mad tune.

There were clowns, a juggler, and an acrobat churning up the dust as he did handsprings and cartwheels. And there were girls—furnished, it was rumored, by Harvey Whent—who cheered, shouted, and now and again broke into song as, arm in arm, they danced along to a fancy step.

But the center of attraction finally came in the person of Marshal Noble Studley, cutting a tough, smart little buckskin down the street; that choppy mustang stepping sideways, with the marshal reining his head high with a real tight grip so he couldn't get his head down to buck and get rid of that load on his back. Buck, for

sure, didn't like the noise, the firecrackers, the drum and
horns and all the rest of it, but Marshal Studley had been
born on a mustang and knew one end of a horse from
the other.

Clint hadn't been absolutely certain, but he would have
bet Studley had polished his tin star; at least it was shining as he rode straight as an Indian—almost—right down
the street, looking neither to right nor left. The news that
the marshal planned to run for mayor had been let out,
and so the citizens were eyeing that former top gunhand
with new interest.

Clint enjoyed every minute of it, though he didn't
lose his vigilance where the Colonel was concerned.
Whenever Witherspoon-Witherspoon moved, the Gunsmith moved right along with him. The magnificent
firelight from the torches showed up the sweat on the
faces of the parading men, while the banging of the big
drum, the sudden clash of cymbals, which was a fresh
surprise, the children darting in and out of the parade
with firecrackers, throwing them without shame into the
ranks of the marchers, all brought the excitement close
to a crescendo.

At one point a firecracker thrown at the feet of the marshal's tough buckskin pony caused him to start to buck.
But Studley was more than handy in that moment that the
Gunsmith thought might surely upend everything with a
riot of laughter. He gripped his reins, holding Buck's
head up, so he could only crowhop.

"Christ, that'll call for a new pair of balls for sure,"
an old-timer remarked loudly within everybody's hearing; and this did bring a surge of laughter. But it swiftly turned to cheers as the veteran in the saddle handled

that tough pony. Even dour-faced Studley was moved to acknowledge the cheering by touching his forefinger to the brim of his big hat.

The parade lasted and lasted until exhaustion set in, and the next morning dawned on a solemn but not necessarily righteous or repentant Plains. Indeed, Clint Adams had discovered that a good time had been had by just about everyone between the ages of six and ninety.

He had said as much as he walked into the office of the *Plains Endeavor*—after knocking.

And so the two men sat there discussing the situation that would maintain now that Plains, it appeared, had won out as county seat.

"I have heard of you, Mr. Adams," the Colonel was saying. "Your reputation as a master of the six-gun and as a man of fair play has preceded you even to this tiny hamlet on the Great Frontier." He leaned forward, his crafty eyes directly on his visitor. "I see clearly that this news pleaseth thee not!" And he sat back, scratching the inside of his thigh.

"I am a man who values privacy, Colonel."

"I realize that, sir. And let me tell you it is a pleasure to have somebody walk into this office who isn't after getting his name in the newspaper. But you want something, I am sure."

"Yes," Clint said quietly. "I want something. But at the same time, I know that you want something. And from me."

He had taken a bold stroke, and he watched it strike the other man.

He realized he had scored when the Colonel said,

"How about a mug of coffee, Mr. Adams? I would favor it. How about yourself?"

It hadn't taken the Great Editor long to switch from coffee to booze; the early hour making no problem. And his guest could do no more than join him.

"Excepting, it isn't going to be so easy," the Colonel was now saying as he regarded the ash on his long cigar, holding it up to his eyes as he leaned an elbow on the arm of his easy chair.

"But I've been hearing that Plains had the whole thing wrapped up," Clint said. "Wasn't that the point of the parade? A celebration of victory?"

Colonel Corliss Witherspoon-Witherspoon cleared his throat; it sounded to Clint like a wagonload of gravel being emptied off its endgate. "Uh, possibly a bit premature. For sure, it does *look* like Plains, but there is still resistance in Mile Butte. Some mean fighting, in point of fact."

"I thought, uh, Mr. Curfew Bakertone had it all sewed up," Clint said, suddenly deciding on a bold move.

The Colonel didn't bat an eye. "For sure, Bakertone offered some time ago to buy up the town of Mile Butte and consolidate it with Plains. But the people in Butte didn't want it on account of—so it is being said—they figured Plains was only a boom town and would soon enough just vanish from the prairie." He shrugged and reached for his drink.

"So it didn't," said Clint, filling in.

"It didn't. Matter of fact, with the immigration coming into the West, folks evidently got hooked on Bakertone's publicity and they mostly headed for Plains; and, liking what they found, they stayed and built their homes."

"And yourself?" Clint asked carefully. "Yourself and the *Endeavor*. Did you see Plains as a building community and feel there was a need for your paper?"

The Colonel beamed. Clearly the Gunsmith had struck the right note.

"This house here, Adams, is the third business house built in the town. No, the second. So I have roots here, sir. Roots. But it hasn't been easy. You read the *Endeavor*, do ya?"

"I do. And I have taken note of the threats and the violence and all the occasions you mention."

The Colonel seemed to straighten in his chair. "Why, all kinds of threats reached me, Adams, specially on account of the *Endeavor* and our speaking so well in favor of Plains. But let me tell you, sir, that I sent word back to those rapscallions that it takes two to make a shooting match. And by Harry, I was ready!"

Clint grinned at him, wondering how much of what he was telling was true. He had heard of the violence, the threats, the pressure coming from Mile Butte. But lately it had simmered down. Yet Witherspoon-Witherspoon seemed to feel that the trouble wasn't totally settled, even though it looked to the Gunsmith, and everyone else he'd heard on the subject, that Plains had won.

"See, we had a sort of election about a year back," the Colonel was saying. "Bakertone pushed for it. Him and the New England Company, that is, backing him. Well, Bakertone, he felt pretty confident he controlled the votes in the northern part of Bullock County because he'd given a lot of the farmers work on his various projects. Thought he'd win. And everybody in Plains was all set up. Figured Plains was as good as the county seat."

"But something went wrong?" Clint said, just to fill in as his host paused for refreshment. Hank Sayles had told him about the abortive election.

"Well, one morning word came that Hawkins Township, which had eighty votes, had said to hell with Bakertone—that is, their leaders had—and the news of maybe getting the railroad through; they wanted cold cash for their votes. They wanted eight thousand dollars for their eighty votes. Well, the men in Plains refused, and the Hawkins boys went and sold their votes to Mile Butte; excepting they wanted the money in advance. But that worked out. Or so it seemed. Anyway, to cut a long story short, Bakertone got wind of it, and next thing anybody knew the voting went through and Plains had won, except that it went to the state supreme court and was proven illegal. So we were back where we started. And now we won again."

"So then there's no problem," Clint said. "Plains is the county seat and the party's over. All over but the shouting."

"Except it isn't, Mr. Adams. There are voices claiming the election was rigged and should be void."

Clint could only shrug at that bit of news. And he did so, smiling amiably at his host.

A silence fell, while each turned to his own thoughts. It was just at that moment that Clint Adams closed in on it.

"There is the smell of a rodent somewhere," he said. "And I feel that is what you have been saying, Colonel."

"If you are as fast with the trigger as you are with your

perception, young man, you'll live a long and healthy life." And Colonel Witherspoon-Witherspoon was beaming all over his shiny face.

Clint nodded toward the newspaper that was lying in front of the Colonel. "Is it in there?"

"No. It is not. And mind, I am not saying anything as to what it is that isn't in the next issue of the *Endeavor*. I too prefer to die of old age."

"I see."

"And so, I have been interviewing you for a story on the Gunsmith." He held up the palm of his hand suddenly to block the words that were already forming in his guest's mind. "Never fear, Adams. I am not printing a word about you."

"Then . . . "

"Then why have I accepted your company here in my office? Since there doesn't appear to be anything that the two of us would have in common, eh?"

"I don't think you have to go any further, Colonel," Clint said, standing up. "I appreciate what you've told me. But as far as writing anything about me; a lot of people have thought of that one, either promising or threatening, almost always for their own benefit, their own plan. You can do what you like about that, mister. I don't give a good or a bad goddamn!"

The Colonel, flushed to almost the color of scarlet, had risen full speed to his feet, almost stumbling as he did so; he was certainly no longer young. "Sir, I have given you absolutely the wrong impression! What I am simply saying is that I wish you would help clear up this mess. A number of us here in Plains feel threatened, and I for one am even extremely cautious about even mentioning any name. But you know who I refer to. There has been bloodshed, and there is likely to be more. You, sir, are a man well versed in the art of gunmanship. We need you. I—the Free Press of the American West—needs you! But I shall not press my point. I have stepped too far over the line, and I beg your forgiveness. I apologize. Colonel Corliss Witherspoon-Witherspoon apologizes most humbly!"

"That's really not necessary, Colonel. As long as we understand each other." Clint was beginning to feel a certain compassion for the old bounder, who, despite everything, revealed a trait of something or other at least approaching honesty. Besides, he was an amiable one. Likable, in spite of his larcenous soul.

"A question, Colonel, which I believe I know the answer to, but I am saying it anyway. With a company like the New England Cattle, Land and Transportation behind you, and especially with a man like Curfew Bakertone heading the operation, how could there be even the thought of a problem as to Plains winning the county seat? It makes no sense. I do know the answer, but I would like to hear you say it."

The Colonel's lips moved back and forth, as though he were trying to locate some morsel of food or possibly a random flake of tobacco. "Of course. Of course! You're saying that with all that behind you, how could you possibly come out second."

Clint said nothing. He simply stood there with his eyes full on the Colonel.

"Sometimes it's necessary to lose," Witherspoon-Witherspoon said. "It happens all the time at cards."

"Right. There is always a winner and a loser, but sometimes there is the factor of the house, yes? And the House always wins." Clint kept his eyes steady on the other man as he spoke, driving his point home.

"We do understand each other," the Colonel said. "That we do." And he placed his palms together, flat as though ready for prayer, and then raised the points of his fingers to his chin. "We are in accord; we understand each other."

"I do understand you, Colonel," Clint said, his words coming out like a fresh deal. "I just hope you understand me."

"I do. I do, sir."

The Gunsmith stood there looking at him, as though sizing him. Which, in fact, he was doing.

"Colonel," the Gunsmith said slowly, "can you tell me just why anybody would really give a damn whether or not Plains or Mile Butte is or is not the county seat of Bullock County?" He paused for just a second and then added, "Other than, as we say in poker, the House?"

The Colonel looked nonplussed at that. Finally, a wry smile appeared at the corners of his mouth. He was about to speak, when suddenly there was the sound of heavy footsteps on the boardwalk outside, and the door opened.

It was Marshal Noble Studley who walked in.

"Heerd you was here, Adams."

"This is where I am," the Gunsmith said easily, suddenly alert to the tension he heard in Studley's voice.

Witherspoon-Witherspoon started to splutter, mumbling something about charging into an office without knocking, etcetera, but neither Clint nor Studley were listening.

"There is trouble," Studley said, his face hard as a

hammer. "Just got word from Mile Butte that they aim to keep their records over there, just so long as their town hall is standing."

"The fools!" The words burst from the Colonel, and he literally snorted. "They can't do that! They lost the election—both times! That by jingo proves the point! They can't keep those records; they have got to come here!"

"Colonel, they are doing it. They are keeping their records in Mile Butte, and you know what they have told Plains to do about it."

"Well, that's up to the town council." The words came blustering out of the Colonel's quivering lips.

"That is exactly why I am here," Marshal Studley said. "I have just spoke with the council, and they want Adams here to go with me to get them records and bring 'em to here."

Clint had known it was coming. And he had his answer ready. He was already shaking his head, even before Studley had finished speaking.

"Sorry, Marshal."

"I can't git deputies, Adams. You know how that is. Everybody's a hero till it's necessary to actually be one."

"I know that. Why not call the army?"

"That would take forever," snapped Colonel Witherspoon-Witherspoon. "Forever! Adams, reconsider. There will be bloodshed. Your presence can avert that. Possibly," he added, looking into the middle distance.

"He's right," Studley said. "There's big trouble. It ain't just the Butte people, but there is a lot of extra people in on it."

"What do you mean by that?" Clint asked. "Who? What do you mean by 'extra people'?"

"Gunmen is who I mean. Some of the riffraff you see down in the cabbage patch who bin slipping into town this past week."

Clint nodded. He had indeed noticed a few "extra" hard-lookers in town. "Are you figuring somebody's stirring trouble, Marshal? That the excitement isn't just because of the county-seat contest?"

"I do."

"And I do too, sir!" said the Colonel, nodding his head so vigorously his wattles quivered. "And Adams, that is precisely why you must assist Marshal Studley."

The Gunsmith had been standing, and now he sat down suddenly.

"You got to help!" Studley insisted.

"When do you figure to ride over to Mile Butte?" Clint asked. And he watched the relief sweep into Studley's face; and the Colonel's, too.

"Tomorrow," Studley said.

"Tomorrow?" repeated the Colonel. "Why not right now, sir?"

"Tomorrow's Sunday," Clint said. "Reckon the marshal figures the boys will be sleeping off their drunks."

"You'll be with us, then?" Studley bent his head toward the Gunsmith.

The Gunsmith was watching the suspense on Witherspoon-Witherspoon's face.

Suddenly there was a scratching at the door that led into a room in back of the office, and the Colonel crossed to it and let in the cat.

Clint waited while the Colonel returned to where he had been standing before his cat had scratched for admittance.

"So you'll be with us?" Studley said again. "We'll be riding at dawn. I've got a couple of men. We'll need a wagon for all the stuff."

The Gunsmith had remained where he was seated. Now he turned his eyes fully onto Marshal Noble Studley, who was standing there with his question still on his face.

"You can tell Mr. Curfew Bakertone, Studley, that I will be there."

He stood up quickly and walked to the door, opened it, and stepped out onto the boardwalk. He looked about him. It was a bright, clear blue morning. There were hardly any people about. And the sun was shining. But there was still today and there was plenty to do, without very much time for it.

Chapter Nine

When he spotted the rangy dun horse at the hitching rack outside the Ever & Always Best Saloon, the Gunsmith felt a strange sense of half-recognition run through him. He knew for a fact that he hadn't laid eyes on the animal before; certainly not directly. So it must have been a streaking glance, the horse maybe in the background some place or other. At the ZT ranch? At the gather? Maybe in town?

Then when he walked into the saloon and saw the range coat lying over the back of a chair, something clicked.

"I bin looking for you," the voice said, coming up behind him. "Figured you'd hit town ere too long."

"Figured the same for yerself," the Gunsmith said, as he turned to face Hank Sayles.

"Take a seat," the big man said, scratching into his head of thick red hair. He waved to the bartender to bring over another glass.

"Ain't no waiting service in this here place, mister." It was the pear-shaped O'Casey in back of the bar. "It's just as far from you to me as t'is from me to you."

"Sure enough." Hank laughed goodnaturedly, and he got up and walked to the bar and picked up the glass.

"Good to see you, Clint," he said, returning to the table.

The Gunsmith said nothing; he was simply looking at his friend, the land surveyor. Suddenly there was an awkward silence. Clint did nothing to change it; and as he continued to sit there without speaking, he could feel Hank's discomfort growing.

Finally his friend reached over, picked up the bottle, and poured into the fresh glass.

When he put the bottle down, he said, "Clint—"

"Yeah. That's my name," said the Gunsmith.

"When did you figure it out?"

Clint reached into his shirt pocket and took out the button he'd found on the trail near the ZT, when the trio of Butch and his two buddies had been so interested in tracking him. When he dropped it onto the table, Hank reached for it.

"Looks like the one I picked up at Vicksburg."

"Did the dun have a loose shoe that day you cut my trail?" Clint asked, nodding slightly toward the swinging doors of the saloon.

"I wanted to talk to you. I mean, bad. But those three ZT owlhooters were too close. Then—then I guess I got cold feet. I wanted to a couple of times."

"You can talk to me now," Clint said.

Hank was leaning on his forearms on the table, holding his glass of whiskey loosely between his two hands. "I guess, like I said, I lost my guts. Didn't want to lose a friend."

"There is something more important than a friend," Clint said quietly.

"What's that?"

"Yourself."

Hank's head bobbed a couple of times in agreement.

"How did they hook you?" Clint asked.

"My wife. Millie. I married couple years after we'd ridden together, you and me. Well, we were real, real happy. Then Millie took sick. Like to died. She didn't, but she's bedridden. But not before I'd gone into big debt." He stopped, locked for the moment in some aspect of memory.

Clint said, "So they got you."

"Bakertone heard about my situation and Millie's illness. And he had the thing I needed—the money—and he even knew of a place to send her. She is there now. They take good care of her."

"Got'cha."

"So they got me. And then I wrote you. Half the time I wanted you to come, and then I didn't. Took me a while to send the letter. Then, when I followed you, I wanted to—to talk, I guess. Anyhow, I can't go through with it. Clint, they've got you set up. I can't—I can't do that."

"I know," Clint said, looking right at the other man, who was now facing him squarely for the first time since they'd sat down.

"You know?" Hank's surprise was great.

Clint nodded.

"How? They didn't tell you anything. How could you have known?"

"I know a man like yourself, Hank, wouldn't be going through the hell you've been living if it wasn't something big, something not of any small order. Not cheap, is what I am saying."

"But how did you know—or did you?—that they were setting you up?"

"First, I know Noble Studley didn't get to be marshal of Plains by dealing his own hand. And he was just too damn eager for me to ride over to Mile Butte with him." He reached into his shirt pocket for his tobacco sack and papers. "You know anything about Witherspoon?"

"Only that he can outtalk any man within the limits of this here country of North America."

"Is he working for Bakertone?"

"I don't think so. Least not directly. You know, of course, that a lot of folks work for Curfew Bakertone without even knowing that's what they're doing."

"Including his wife?"

"More than likely, I'd say."

"And what about Slade? Is he in on it?"

Hank took a pull at his drink. "No. But he is in the way."

"And the MM?" He was thinking of Tony and Andy Miller.

"Not according to my reckoning. No, the land Bakertone is after is right smack in the ZT domain."

"That is what I figured. However, anything happens there, it's bound to bear on the Miller place."

"And some others too. Bakertone and company will want to spread themselves."

"For sure." Clint nodded in agreement, as his thoughts tallied the possibilities, the effects of the big coup that was being planned by the Bakertones and the New England Company.

"Thing I can't yet figure," Hank said, "is why he didn't just plan a fake gold rush, salt a couple of mines. This here is complicated."

"You know the answer to that one, Hank."

Sayles nodded. "Yeah; guess I do."

The Gunsmith was shaking his head slowly as he pondered it.

"Gold. You'd have everybody for a thousand miles around pouring in here."

"But Bakertone's got a lot of people already wondering if there isn't gold still about. There've been plenty of hints."

"Hints that were planted so's they'd be squashed," Clint said. "No. Gold is too simple. In a way, too easy. Water is different. Water you can control. And while it's more important than gold, for sure, it is gold that drives men crazy."

"Well, you hit the jackpot there, my friend." Hank scratched his head suddenly. "There is a lot of water under one section of the ZT range. A whole lot of water. And Asa Slade doesn't have a notion of it."

"What about those three gunhawks he's got there? That feller they call a deputy foreman. They know?"

"Might. Of course, they were shoved onto Asa by Bakertone. And they've caused a helluva lot of ruckus rustling cattle and even horses. Making trouble, see, with the MM and the other outfits around, so that they'll fight each other and be more easy to take over."

"But how did Bakertone get wind of it? How did he learn there was water?"

Hank's face whitened considerably as he paused over Clint's question. "I told him. He'd first heard it from someone who'd heard it from the Indians. And since I owed him lock, stock, and barrel, he had me survey. I proved up on it. There's a whole lake down there."

"But not on the MM range," Clint said, wanting again to verify the position of Tony and her young brother.

"No. It's north of the MM. And west. Of course, anyone wanting the water would likely want the MM range as well."

Another silence fell between them now. Then Clint reached for his glass, took a drink, and put the glass down slowly.

The silence lengthened as the two men sat there, each with his thoughts. Clint was going over all of it, from the very beginning, when he'd first received Hank's letter. All the pieces had fallen into place. Funny, how his thoughts found it now. He'd been feeling it almost from the beginning. The sense that something was off, really off, but not something that he could actually see and name. His thoughts had been like clouds, formless and drifting, but then every once in a while coming together into a pattern of some kind. And though still vague, he'd been getting the impression that there was more to what he was looking at, more than the simple eye was taking in. And then all that vagueness sharpened, came into focus, and began to appear in a form that, even without any logical argument, he knew was right.

The Gunsmith felt the whole scramble of thought leave him like a great load that had been dumped; and he felt light, clear, and he knew exactly what he was going to do.

When he raised his head, he found that Hank was looking at him.

"How is she?" Clint asked. "How is Millie?"

He would never forget the expression that came into Hank's big face as he said, "She is wonderful!"

Clint Adams was gambling that his move to join forces with Marshal Noble Studley would throw Bakertone off balance. At least for the moment. And seeing his way more clearly in regard to Hank Sayles and how his friend had become so seriously involved with Bakertone, he felt he could rely on Hank's loyalty. It was a load off him to realize this, and as the day broke with his stepping out into the street in front of the K. C. House, he knew that it was the moment when everything would be decided.

He had coffee and sourdough biscuits, plus a steak as an afterthought, at the Gentle Cafe, rather than in his hotel. He wanted to be alone while he thought through his strategy for the day's action. He knew he'd have enough people around him soon enough. And he appreciated the half-hour to himself as he sat in the deserted cafe with the sunlight now touching the dirty windowpanes.

When Hank walked in, he explained what he wanted him to do. "You watch from the rooftops," he said. "Of course, keeping out of sight yourself."

"You'll be riding with Studley?"

"And whoever else is with him. But I want you out of it; I mean as far as Bakertone and his boys are concerned. Of course, if you see anything or anybody special, then let me hear it."

Hank nodded. "Play it as it happens."

"It's the best way," Clint said.

His friend grinned suddenly. "Don't you plan things ahead? I used to wonder about that in the old days."

"I only make a plan so's I can change it."

"Huh?" Hank scratched into his head of thick red hair.

"If you don't have a plan in the first place," Clint explained, "then you don't have anything to change from. See?"

"I guess I do," Hank said with a shy grin.

It was an expression Clint Adams had only once before seen on his friend's face. And that was recently, when he'd asked how Millie was and Hank had told him she was "wonderful." Something had definitely changed for Hank Sayles, and Clint was glad.

Five minutes later they had finished their breakfast, and each had gone his own way.

At the livery, Clint found the hostler waiting for him. He was an old-timer named Elihu, stove up some but still handy at running the stable.

"That big black horse of yours," Elihu said as he watched the Gunsmith's approach from the doorway of his establishment.

"What about him?" Clint asked, feeling something tighten in his guts. Then it loosened as he acknowledged it.

"Couple fellers walked in just a while back, askin' about leaving some hosses here and how much I'd charge 'em."

He paused to let fly a thick streak of brown saliva, and then, his jaws working again on his chew, he said, "Big, heavyset feller and a thin one with a busted snout. I seen 'em once before in Moriarty's a while back. They was lookin' at your hoss."

"That all? Just looking?"

"They were telling what a piece of horseflesh the black was and how the big feller would give a lot to own him."

"You mean, saying it so's you could hear it," Clint said.

The old boy's eyes widened. "Yeah, that is correct! How'd you know that?"

"Figured."

He led Duke out into the middle of the livery and slipped his bridle on, then the saddle blanket, and finally the stock saddle he'd had with him since almost he couldn't remember. Except he could. He'd bought it in Fort Worth one day after pulling in a big pot at the Lucky Deal. That had been quite a game. Luke Short had been there.

The sun was well into the morning sky as he rode up the main street to join Studley and his bay saddlehorse, plus the two-horse team and box wagon and the marshal's "deputy," a gent named Chip Fingers, who had recently spent time in the town's log jail—which consisted of a single thick log and a stout chain, which were kept in an open shed behind the marshal's office. Chip had allegedly been caught cheating at cards and had only escaped the ultimate reward for such action by the sudden appearance of the marshal, who rescued him for later "trial." Since all of the players, including Chip, were sloshed to full capacity with trail whiskey, no one was able to offer any sound objection. Now the prisoner had been offered a chance at "probation," since the search for deputies had once again shown Marshal Studley what he already knew: that the situation was hopeless.

"I'd like to swear you in as deputy, Adams," was the first thing he said as Clint rode up.

"Marshal, let's cut the cackle and cut leather. We got a day's work ahead of us."

The marshal, seeing the look in the Gunsmith's face, offered no argument.

At a nod from Marshal Studley, Chip Fingers clucked to his team and the party started across the plain toward Mile Butte.

After a while, Studley pulled up closer to the Gunsmith and said, "If we do get separated, Chip'll have the wagon waiting at the courthouse, and we'll head back for Plains on the south side of the river."

The streets of Mile Butte were deserted as they rode in and pulled up in front of the two-story brick building in which the office of the acting county clerk was located.

Clint followed Studley into the building, wondering where Hank Sayles was. Hank would have followed them and cut around before they'd reached Mile Butte, to enter from another direction. Any time now, he could find a place where he could cover Clint and Studley and Chip—although neither Studley nor Chip knew of that plan. Clint was still pretty sure of Studley still being a Bakertone man.

At the same time, he was counting on the fact that the Mile Butte and Plains people were fairly fed up with gunfighting and would probably not come out in any kind of force. The signs all pointed to a local fight: that is, the Bakertone bunch simply taking over the town records now that Plains was the county seat in actual fact. Or was it? It was the uncertainty, Clint realized, that added the extra twist to the situation. Everybody was screwed up pretty damn tight, especially those who were involved with the possibilities of power and special favors. But since the lines weren't so clearly drawn to the public, at any rate, the action as Clint saw it was focusing on himself, plus Studley and Bakertone's owlhooters, more than probably including Butch Holmes and his two buddies, Hymes and Donnicker.

"That's Jeff Hennessey," Studley said, as he and the Gunsmith walked into the office, and he already had the man at the desk covered.

"We're taking the records," Studley said. "You can start carrying them out."

At this point Chip came in, and together the two men piled up the books, while Studley got the seal so that they couldn't issue any more script. Clint also picked up a load of books and started for the door, where he shifted the load into his left arm so that his right was free if needed.

They threw the books into the wagon box. They had just started back when the first six-shooter went off—five shots, right in a row. This was followed by a roar of buckshot that raked the building.

"They're not aiming to hit us! Only scare us off!" Studley shouted to Clint and Chip.

But the Gunsmith was already signaling his two companions to get back into the building. "That's just the beginning," he explained when they were back in the office. "Somebody tipped them off that we were coming. But they're also not trying to kill us. Yet."

"How the hell you figger that?" snapped Studley.

"It's obvious. It's been obvious all along what Bakertone and his gang want," Clint said.

"What? What the hell do you mean?" Studley was glaring at him, his eyes hard as nails.

"They want me. But they want me alive. If they drygulch me, they'll never make it in Plains or Mile Butte."

"You're crazy!" Studley said.

But at that point somebody came running into the building. It was Hank Sayles, and he was carrying a Winchester. Shots followed him, but nobody had seemed too interested in hitting him.

"Jesus, it isn't any too friendly out there," he said.

"They're Bakertone men, aren't they?" Clint said. "They're not Butte people shooting at us."

"That's the size of it."

"Good enough. Just so we know who we're dealing with. Now we've got this clerk here as hostage. What's your name, mister? You're Jeff Hennessey?"

The clerk was obviously scared. His face was very white, his hands were trembling. "That's not our men out there, mister. For sure. We ain't aiming to have any more bloodshed over who gets to be county seat."

"Looks like Bakertone's men have took over," Studley said.

"It does." The Gunsmith's words were soft.

"What you reckon we can do, Adams?"

"That's an easy one, Marshal. Why don't you just mosey out there and arrest them." And while the lawman's jaw dropped, Clint said over his shoulder to Hank Sayles, "Can you get up on the roof without going outside?" And he moved his hand toward the clerk. "Hennessey! You show him!"

"I can." The clerk had recovered some of his nerve, though now as a pane of glass suddenly cracked open from a load of buckshot, he blanched considerably.

A shout followed. "You men come on out! Studley!"

"Shit," Studley said.

By then Hank and Hennessey had already disappeared. Clint waited, giving them time to get onto the roof and for Hank to settle into a good spot with his Winchester.

"Chip, you cover us from the corner of that window there. Take my Winchester there."

"What you gonna use?"

"That is a dumb question," the Gunsmith said.

"Adams, you ain't going out there!" The alarm in Studley's voice sounded genuine. "Alone!"

"No," said the Gunsmith. "You're going with me."

They stood facing each other then, and Clint watched the other man's fingers twitch. "Out there, Studley. You don't want to draw on me in here."

"What the hell you talkin' about!" But Studley's face had gone dead white.

"Studley . . . after you. No one's going to throw down on you. And in fact, I'll be right behind you to make sure they don't."

The marshal of Plains seemed to be rooted to the spot.

"Tell me something, Studley." The Gunsmith said those words slowly, almost as though he were weighing each one. And now as he spoke, his tone was even more paced with something that meant more than just what was being said: "Why did you kill your brother?"

Studley's eyes flickered. Clint Adams again felt how very strange those eyes were. "Prior drew on me, that's why. Family squabble. He'd of kilt me if I hadn't been faster."

"Faster than him—than your brother—you're saying?"

Studley nodded. "That is correct." And then he added, "That was the way of it."

The Gunsmith waited another moment or two, listening to the group of men outside. They had quieted down, because somebody had called out that there were two rifles covering them from the roof.

"We'll go now," the Gunsmith said. "You lead the way. You're the law. Me, I'm just somebody passing through."

For just a second Studley hesitated, but then he turned and started out the door. The Gunsmith followed.

There were a good dozen men in the group standing around the team and wagon. But they were no longer shouting. Yet, Clint could see they were nevertheless restive.

"Here they come!" A shout or two went up, but then a charged silence fell. It seemed to encompass the entire street, even the town. And as Clint Adams and Marshal Noble Studley stepped off the boardwalk, the group opened up, but didn't lose its tension.

Somebody said something, but the Gunsmith saw it was nothing of importance. He had stopped a few feet from the boardwalk, but with good clearance, so that if necessary he could maneuver without bumping into the wooden walk. Right off he had spotted Butch Holmes and his buddies, Hymes and Donnicker. He cut a quick look at Duke, standing at the hitching rack well away from the group.

"So tell them, Marshal." Clint's words were quiet, but they were heard by all in the clear morning air.

"We'll be taking the town records and such over to Plains, since it's now the county seat," Studley said, addressing the group.

No one said anything to this. Out of the side of his eye, Clint saw Butch Holmes moving slowly away from the edge of the group.

"Stay where you are," he called out.

"Who you talkin' to, Gunsmith?" It was Mint Donnicker speaking from the other side of the waiting group, which was now opening even more.

"I'm talking to that hog-fat sonofabitch not to move one inch closer to my horse. I mean right now!"

Donnicker struck for his sidearm, but a shout from the rooftop brought him to a freeze, as Hank Sayles covered him with the Winchester.

But Butch Holmes was not so lucky. He had his gun free of its holster when the Gunsmith, smooth as grease, drew and shot him right between the eyes.

"Gunsmith!"

Clint Adams had been waiting for it, and he turned, dropped to the ground, and shot Studley—who had been standing behind him—in his guts.

"Holy Mother of God!" somebody murmured, loud enough for one or two of the spectators to hear.

The Gunsmith was on his feet in a jiffy and standing over the gun-shot Marshal Studley.

"Never, never would of figgered . . . so fast . . . " The words tumbled out of the dying man's mouth. "You . . . h-had . . . back to . . . me . . . "

"Like Noble," the Gunsmith said. "Noble had his back to you too, didn't he, Prior? Cute, taking your brother's name."

He knelt down then as Prior Studley's eyes closed forever, and he removed the marshal's badge.

When he stood up again, Hank was standing beside him. Clint handed him the badge. "I think you ought to be acting marshal, Hank. At least till they maybe pick somebody else. Meantime, somebody's got to get this cleaned up and straighten things out with the two towns. First person I'd suggest you talk to is Colonel Witherspoon-Witherspoon."

"Holy smokes!" Hank Sayles said, scratching his red head. "And then what?"

"Why, like we both decided, remember? You let what's going to happen, happen."

As he walked toward the big black horse, Duke turned his head and snorted. Clint unwrapped the reins from the hitching rack. "You know," he said, "that big feller did say one right thing, even so: You are, by golly, a fine-looking horse!"

"But how could you just make your friend the marshal like that?" Tony asked him a few hours later. "Doesn't that take a judge or the army or another marshal or someone like that? Someone with some kind of big authority?"

"Well, it's like this," Clint explained, having a difficult time keeping his thoughts on the conversation. "See, they wanted me to act as a marshal—marshal or acting marshal, that's to say—and I refused. I didn't want that. I'd been a lawman, and, well, I didn't want it again. But then, since there wasn't any lawman around after Studley got shot, then I figured somebody had to take charge, and it seemed I was the right one for that. You follow me?"

She nodded. They were sitting together on the horsehair sofa in her living room after supper, and he'd been
telling her all about the action at Mile Butte, as well
as some things about Plains and Asa Slade and Curfew
Bakertone.

"So, since I was a sort of acting marshal—or could
have been considered as such—I figured I could pass
the tin on to Hank."

"I see. But now what about Slade and what about
Bakertone and all his scheming? What's going to happen
there?"

He reached for his mug of coffee and took a swallow.
"You sure make a mighty nice cup of coffee, ma'am."

"Let's stay on the subject, sir."

He grinned at her, feeling the warmth coming from
her, feeling himself opening just the way she was doing;
and he didn't want to talk about all that had happened.
He wanted . . . Well, why not get it out of the way and
done with, he was thinking.

"Hank is a licensed, highly respected surveyor. He's
going to the army and the government with a report on
the water situation and full details on how Bakertone tried
to ramrod Asa Slade by blackmailing him into taking
gunmen who were switching brands and rustling not
only cattle but horses. And also how he tried rigging the
county-seat election so's his company—meaning himself—could control the whole Horseshoe Valley section.
Plus getting Prior Studley appointed marshal through
bribery. Hank's making a clear sweep of his own part
in the affair, and they'll believe him. He sure had plenty
of extenuating reasons for what he almost did. Except
when it got down to the nub, he just couldn't. That's

why he came to me." He paused, looking at her. "That do it?"

"I guess so. Phew! That was a big mouthful you gave me for a simple question."

"Well, you asked for it. I've got—"

"I have one more question."

"Yeah? What?"

"What will happen to Asa Slade?"

"Dunno. Except I could guess."

"What?"

"Asa will for sure go on being Asa."

She laughed at that, her face lighting up, and he felt his excitement mounting.

"One thing more."

"It's got to be the last thing, miss."

"Fair enough. But . . . Well, maybe I won't ask it. It's too personal."

He could tell that she was funning, and it delighted him. "Come on. Out with it."

"If you make Hank an acting marshal, then what does that make you?" She said it with full seriousness, but he could see the twinkle in her eye, and he could sure feel what else was going on with her.

"What does that make me? Why, that makes me an acting lover," he said. "That should be clear." And he slipped his arm around her.

"I'm sorry, but I can only settle for a full-fledged lover," she whispered, hardly able to finish her sentence, as he slid his hand up under her dress.

The Gunsmith had no trouble reaching his destination. "Boy, I'm glad that question is settled," he said.

TRACKER *series*
by
Award-Winning Author
Robert J. Randisi (J.R. Roberts)

Visit us at www.speakingvolumes.us

MOUNTAIN JACK PIKE *series*
by
Award-Winning Author
Robert J. Randisi (J.R. Roberts)

Visit us at www.speakingvolumes.us

ANGEL EYES *series*
by
Award-Winning Author
Robert J. Randisi (J.R. Roberts)

Visit us at

www.ingramcontent.com/pod-product-compliance
Lightning Source LLC
Chambersburg PA
CBHW020636250626
47154CB00008B/2702